BACK AT THE RANCH

THE MCCOYS:
BEFORE THE FEUD
BOOK 3

THOMAS A. MCCOY

ISBN 978-1-7327827-1-6 (paperback)

PROLOGUE

As soon as the last light went out in the farmhouse, Tommy saddled his horse and walked him quietly out of the barn. He didn't mount up until he was sure they were far enough away that they wouldn't be heard. He took up a fast pace, but not so fast as to burn up his horse. He figured he had twenty miles to cover to get to their camp and had to use the same horse for the ride back.

Jeb was on watch. As he saw Tommy approaching, he hollered to the others and they all got out of their bedrolls to find out what had happened.

Tommy filled them in on the situation. Then looking directly at his pa, he said, "You need to be on that side road that's about ten miles downriver, the one that comes over the hill to meet the river road, by around two o'clock. You'll need a horse saddled and ready, trailing the wagon."

He turned to A.C. and Oliver and said, "You need to get there early, set up in the trees, and to be ready to start shooting as soon as they approach Pa's wagon." A.C. and Oliver exchanged a glance. Tommy's tone made it clear that their role would be crucial.

"At the first shot," he said to his pa, "you're to jump off the driver's seat into the back of the wagon, grab your horse, and hightail it out of there. Me and Aron will meet y'all back at the campsite as soon as we can." He stood

1

and settled his hat more firmly on his head. "I have to get back before someone notices I'm gone, or I'm sure they'll kill Aron." With that said, he left.

He made it back to the abandoned farmhouse hideout at about three o'clock in the morning. After unsaddling his horse and rubbing it down as best he could, he climbed back into his bedroll to get a couple of hours sleep, but not before he told Aron what the plan was. After the gang stole the wagon, they would have to come with them back to the farmhouse or risk their suspicion.

The next morning the gang was up and about much earlier than Tommy expected. Everyone in one group, they set out to rob Tommy's father.

INTRODUCTION

The McCoys had taken back a good portion of the wealth and gold stolen by northern soldiers from southern families and had given much of it to a church for distribution to those who had lost everything. It seemed they'd gotten away with the raids and would be able to live their lives in peace. One group of their family had decided to go home to Kentucky, to their old homesteads. But because of the gold coins spent to fund this trip, suspicion was cast back on the McCoys still living at the ranch where they'd gone to lay low for a while. When alerted about this change of situation by a telegram sent from the Kentucky-bound McCoys, they knew they had to quickly find a way to protect themselves.

James and Wiley had started sending messages once they'd reached Kentucky. The messages had started out with a cheery tone. One of them included the fact that they had been able to turn their share of the gold into usable money and were making a great life for their families back home. Another helped explain what they had done to their gold in order to claim that it was rightly theirs and was intended, Tommy assumed, as a way to help the McCoys still at the ranch do same. But the last message from Wiley had been different.

Its purpose was to let him know the Pinkertons had

decided to return to Lawrence, Kansas, the place the trail of the gold had originated, and more specifically, their ranch.

That meant the Pinkertons were going to be coming back there and looking all that much harder at all the rest of the McCoys, as well as digging deeper into the story of how Terry had gotten the gold coins they had spent to build the ranch.

The men had grown comfortable on the ranch, and security was lax. They'd kept much of the gold piled up in the barn, where it would be easy for the Pinkertons to find.

When Tommy came back from town after receiving Wiley's last telegram, he told the McCoys about its disturbing contents. "I'm afraid our group is going to have to split up," he said, "even though I've really enjoyed the life we've started, living and working together." He explained the way the Kentucky relatives had been able to turn their gold into usable money, then added, "But it would be too much of a coincidence if we all started finding gold mines." The men agreed.

"I think the best thing for y'all," Tommy continued, "would be to get as far away from the ranch as possible and not spend any of the coins or turn them in to an assayer's office till you get to where you're going. It's going to be risky for everyone to be traveling and carrying all that gold, but I just can't see any other way to try and keep it without getting in trouble. Whatever we do, we need to do it fast because the Pinkertons are on their way back. I doubt if it will take them more than three weeks." To make his point about doing things quickly, Tommy asked for a volunteer to ride out to the others' homes and pass the word along. "Tell them to come here in three days so we can talk about what to do," he said.

For the men, getting comfortable after the raids had also meant starting ranches of their own near Terry's place. After the first McCoys left for Kentucky, three groups had moved to acreage nearby. Unfortunately, they hadn't been able to spend their gold to buy the materials and equipment they needed to build a real house and ranch like Tommy and his family had done. They had only been able to build small shacks to live in and rough sheds to store their farming equipment and the feed and tack for their horses. Their wagons and livestock were housed in a roofed shelter with no walls, a makeshift setup until they could build something better. Overall, their outfits resembled squatters' residences.

The men who had stayed at the ranch were working as ranch hands. They were comfortable in the nice bunkhouse and huge barn that had been built. But this comfort would end if they didn't do something to keep the gold and avoid getting arrested. If arrested and put on trial, they would be hanged. If the Pinkertons found any evidence, the raids would be called a war crime, even though no one had been killed. And worst of all, the arrest of any of them would point to all of the other McCoys who had been at the ranch, and the Pinkertons would do their best to find links to connect them all.

Chapter 1

Coming Up with a Plan

After Tommy stopped at the bunkhouse to tell the other McCoys at the ranch what he had found out, he headed into the house to tell his family. Terry and her sister Patty were in the kitchen making fresh pasta for dinner. When Terry saw him, she took her hands out of the bowl of dough she was working and asked, "What's happened? I can tell how you're looking at me it's not good."

They'd developed a good working relationship since Tommy had come back to the ranch. But Terry had called off their engagement soon after. Her father hadn't returned from war, and she had let him stay on as her partner in the ranch, but she asked him to put a cot in the sitting room by the fireplace to sleep. Sharing a room didn't look good to her family or the men, she told him. But the truth was that she was no longer comfortable sharing a bed with him.

He'd hurt her badly when he'd enlisted in the army despite her protests, and Terry's heart still felt too bruised to risk getting close to him again. She appreciated Tommy's help and told him so. She was trying to trust him enough to let her love for him rekindle, but she secretly doubted they'd ever be able to be together again in a loving sense.

"I got another telegram," Tommy said. "This time from Wiley. He says they managed to get their money in the bank by filing a mining claim like James, but the Pinkertons caught up with them and searched their property, and though there was nothing to find by then, they were mighty suspicious because all the McCoys in his group had found large amounts of gold in their mines. Wiley said the Pinkertons are a private detective agency the general hired to find the gold. They are on their way back here to where they originally picked up the trail of gold coins."

Terry wiped her hands on a towel and sat heavily in a chair.

"We're going to have to do something before they get here," Tommy continued, "and some of us will have to leave if they want to be able to ever use the gold they have. We can't all stay here and be able to spend it, especially not anytime soon. And we can't buy anything more with the gold coins."

Terry nodded. She seemed too calm. "The worst of it," Tommy said, sighing, "is that the men who want to stay here aren't going to be able to if they want to use their gold. At least they'll have only lost some sweat and time from trying to work their land."

Terry stood up and folded her arms.

"So, what do you mean, 'We have to do something?'" she asked.

"Well, I'm saying that we have to get it in a safe place where they won't find it. Then somehow we have to get suspicion off us. I told the men what Wiley said and sent word to the other McCoys at their places. We're going to meet here in three days and talk about what we can do. Whatever it is, we have to do it soon; those Pinkertons will be back within a month. If they find anything, they can put us on trial for war crimes, and that means they could hang us if we're found guilty."

Terry gasped. "Oh my God! You mean they could hang all of us?" she said.

Tommy closed his eyes and nodded. "Yeah," he said, "even though you and your family didn't take part in the raids, you're still accomplices, and that makes you just as guilty."

In her father's absence, Terry had done her best to take care of her brother Jeb and sister Patty, and Tommy's words were making her pray hard that she hadn't put them in jeopardy by allowing his family to shelter there.

"I knew that this had gone over too easy," she said. "I knew they wouldn't just give up looking for all that gold. We've got to find a way to make them decide that we weren't any part of this, only, how are we going to do that? I'm not running away from my home, and I sure don't want to get hanged."

Suddenly, she started to tremble and had to sit down again. "What are we going to do?" she asked. Her voice was high-pitched and frantic. "Have we spent so much money we can't say we got it from the old place Pa sold? Do you think they will just come here and arrest us? Could they put us in jail and hold us there while they look around and search every inch of this ranch for evidence?"

She was working herself into a lather, and Tommy cut her off. "Stop jumping to conclusions," he said. "They can't take us away if they don't have evidence or proof. We just have to make sure they don't find any."

He laid his hand on her shoulder. She flinched a little at his touch. "We need to stay calm and think clearly. I'm going out to the field and tell my dad and Jeb. You just try and calm down and finish doing what you're doing. We'll talk more about it tonight at dinner."

The field his father and Jeb were working wasn't very far away from the house, about a quarter-mile, so he decided he would walk there so he could think. One thought kept turning over and over in his mind: *how could they make the Pinkertons believe the thieves were someone other than the McCoys?*

It was clear that they were going to have to put the blame on someone. He couldn't think of any other way out. He didn't feel good about having someone else pay for a crime they hadn't committed—a crime which to most people of the South wasn't a crime at all, because all they had done was take back what the northern army's own soldiers stole, first from the innocent southern families, and then from the northern army itself. If any crimes had been committed, it had been by those renegade Union Army soldiers who had actually made the initial raids and stashed away the loot they wanted for themselves.

But there was no way they would be able to put the blame on them. Their groups had been disbanded, and the soldiers who'd stayed in the army had been sent to other places.

When he reached the field, he still had no idea what to do. Thomas Sr. put his hay rake on the wagon as Tommy approached. "What are you doing, walking all

9

the way out here?" he said.

"I was hoping I would come up with some kind of an idea," Tommy said.

"What do you mean an idea? An idea for what? What's happened now?" his pa asked.

Tommy told him about his trip to town and the telegram from Wiley.

"So that's what I've been trying to think about," he said, "how to get those Pinkertons looking at somebody else to blame."

His father didn't seem surprised by the news. "Yep," he said, "I'd say that puts us in a pretty bad predicament. This is something I figured would come up sooner or later."

"I've already told the men at the ranch and sent word to the others at their places," Tommy said. "Hopefully, we can come up with some idea that can get those Pinkertons off of us permanently."

His pa nodded. "There is no doubt though that a lot of us are going to have to move somewhere else if we want to use that gold anytime soon," he said.

"Why don't you quit for the day and come back to the house?" Tommy said. "We can start talking about this over dinner. We have to take action quickly." Tommy's pa hailed Jeb, who was on the other side of the field, and as they rode back to the house in the wagon together, nobody said a word.

When the food had been served and Tommy, his pa, Terry and her brother and sister were all sitting at the dinner table, Terry folded her hands together and said she would say grace. She thanked the Lord for the food that was in front of them and for the life they were starting to live. She also asked that he help them find a solution to their problem without any innocent people getting hurt or paying the price for something they didn't do.

This didn't help Tommy's conscience at all. He knew Terry and her family had taken in his family out of the kindness of their hearts. But they'd never been asked if they wanted to be a part of this, even though it was Terry and Patty who had gotten them the information they needed to pull off the raids. He was sure she had directed those words to him.

In reality, Terry had no intention of making him feel guilty. She knew that by allowing the McCoys to stay on the ranch she had become part of what they had done. She was only praying for help in getting out of the situation, without someone who wasn't involved paying a harsh and unfair price.

As they started to eat their supper, Tommy began the discussion. "I think first off, we need to get the gold out of the barn and hide it," he said. "We should probably take it out on the range land and bury it."

Thomas Sr. added that burying it was a good idea, but he thought they should put it out at the end of one of their plowed fields, so that if they ever needed to get to it, it would seem like they were just working in the field. That way, if someone did see them digging, it wouldn't seem out of place, like it would if they were digging on the grazing range. They all agreed that was the better option.

"That's a good idea for us," Tommy said, "but we need to find an idea that works for everyone." There were nods around the table.

"Wiley said that if we needed any money, he would send us some," he continued. "All we had to do was ask. I think I should ask him to send us some money, and we can divide it up between us all. That way, we can spend a bit for what we need, and those who decide they're going to leave will have money to travel with and make a start where they end up. I've done some figger'n', and borrowing sixty-three thousand will give everyone three thousand, including Terry, Patty, and Jeb. That will be plenty of money for everyone to go somewhere and get a new start if they want to and keep going for a few years, if they're careful."

Patty and Terry and Jeb looked relieved at this news. They'd enjoyed the ease of having spending money and weren't looking forward to returning to a hardscrabble life.

"I'll go into town tomorrow and send a telegram to Wiley and ask him to wire the money into an account here at the bank in town," Tommy continued. "All of us will have to go to the bank and open an account. Then those who leave won't have to carry so much cash along with their gold. When they get to a town, they can just go to the bank or telegraph office and have the bank send the money."

Tommy knew this would be asking a lot of some of his kin. Very few of them had ever amassed enough money to have need of a banking system. "I think some of them are talking about going to California," Tommy said. "They'll just have to take their chances carrying the cash and the gold, because the telegraph isn't in a lot of places yet. But at least they won't be leaving a trail by spending those gold coins for the Pinkertons to follow.

I'll tell Wiley how I'm going to divide the money and that everyone will pay back their share to him directly somehow. I'm sure he won't have a problem with doing that for us."

Tommy's pa agreed that it was an excellent idea and should be done right away, as it would take some time to get the money credited at the bank. For a few moments they all sat silently, absorbed in thought, even though their plates were still full. It was all a lot to take in.

Tommy's mind, still consumed with the McCoys being suspects, soon gave them another thing to work over in their heads. "We still need to find a way to get suspicion off us for good. Those of us who stay here are going to have to hold on to the gold for several years before we can start putting any in the bank or filing a mining claim. And when we do start to use it, we can only do it a little at a time; we don't want anyone wondering about us. It will have to look like we got it from something we sold off the ranch—horses, cattle, crops."

He picked up a napkin and wiped his mouth. "You all remember General Thomas Ewing Jr.?" he said. "He was the commander of all those groups of soldiers who had committed raids on the border areas between Kansas and Missouri, and he owned that last place we raided. Well, we also need to get that general satisfied that he's found the people who took the gold so he will quit having the Pinkertons search for it."

Terry, trying to help, asked, "What do we know about this investigation?"

Tommy cleared his throat. "We know that the government has no idea about the gold and didn't hire those Pinkertons, because if they had, that general and those other groups we took the stuff from would be in jail or hanged for war crimes."

All in all, it was a good brainstorming session. Even though the only concrete plan they had come up with was to bury their portion of the gold out at the end of a farm field and to ask Wiley to wire money to the bank in town, everyone stood up from the table feeling they'd made a good start on protecting themselves.

• • •

The next morning, Tommy went into town to send the wire to Wiley. Patty went with him, as she still worked in the Eldridge House as a City Hall secretary's assistant two days a week. She might soon work there three days a week because the city had been growing rapidly since the war ended.

They had tied her horse to the back of the wagon, and at the Eldridge House, she tied it to the hitching rail in front of the building and went into work.

Patty was an assistant to the two full-time secretaries employed at the Eldridge House. She helped them keep up with all of their duties, so she was privileged to information about everything that was going on in town and around the state. She would soon realize just how important some of that information would be.

She was responsible for posting the bulletins that gave notice to the citizens of upcoming events happening within the town and throughout the state. She was also required to take any notices that were to be published in the newspaper to the newspaper office and bring anything directed to the sheriff to him. The wanted posters, which were printed and sent out by the state to all towns came through their office, and she transported them to the sheriff.

It just so happened that the day before, the mail coming in from the stage had contained a stack of wanted posters for gangs of highway robbers up and down the Missouri-Kansas border. Patty was given the stack to take to the sheriff. As she walked to his office, she looked at some of the posters and realized that the men were mostly ex-soldiers who had turned into bandits. This probably happened, she thought, because they had nowhere to go, no home to go back to, and didn't know what they could do for a living, except join a gang.

At that moment an interesting thought occurred to her: what if some of these criminals started spending gold coins?

The posters had the places where these criminals had last been seen printed on the bottom. She decided to go back to the office and write this information down, as well as the number of men in the different areas that were on those posters. She had a sense that it might help them to figure out some sort of plan of action, even if she didn't know how. When she finished, she headed back down the street to the sheriff's office.

At the end of the day, she folded up the papers she had written the information on and stuffed them into her pocket. Smiling to herself, she got on her horse and rode home, thinking she had something that might help them, although she still didn't know how.

When she got to the ranch, Tommy, his pa, and Jeb were still out working in the fields. They'd been trying all day long to think of some way to get the suspicion off of them, but without success. When they finished plowing, they headed back to the ranch together. Patty pulled Tommy aside while the others were washing up for dinner and told him about the posters she had taken to the sheriff that day and the information she'd copied. "What do you think would happen if these men turned up spending gold coins?" she said as she handed him her notes.

Tommy's eyes lit up. She had thought her idea was good, but when she saw his face, she was sure. She knew what had to happen next would be to come up with a way to get the gold into the hands of those criminals without anyone knowing where it had come from.

"We need to figure out how we can use this," Tommy said. "We'll talk about it at dinner again and see if anyone comes up with an idea."

At the dinner table, Tommy said grace. He thanked the Lord for the food, for keeping everyone healthy and safe, and for the idea Patty had thought of, and the information she had gotten. He then asked for help to find a way to make it happen. When he said, "Amen," everyone looked from him to Patty, curious to hear what she'd discovered.

As they were passing the food, Tommy told everyone about the wanted posters.

"If we can find a way to get some of the gold to those bandits and let them spend it wherever they go, that just might be enough to keep us safe," he said.

Thomas Sr. cleared his throat. "That's a good thought," he said, "but we'll all have to give up some of our gold in order to have enough of it get found, so they'll think they found the right men."

Tommy nodded. "We'll also have to find a way that the bandits can't say they got it from us," he said. "We could get the gold to them by letting them find it or steal it from someone on the road. What if we went back to the towns close to where we made the raids and managed to get the highway gangs there enough of the gold to make it seem like several groups were stealing from those stockpiles?"

Terry shook her head. "You can't just drive a wagon into their territory and expect them to steal it from you and not kill you when they find out what's in it. You can't just take a wagon and abandon it there, either; you don't know who might find it. We have to make sure that the bandits that get their hands on it. They're criminals anyway and should be made to pay for the robbing and killing they've already done, but we don't want some innocent traveler to find it and end up going to jail because someone thinks he stole it."

They all agreed that no innocents should get caught up in this, but if real criminals managed to, it was fine. "I couldn't sleep at night," Terry said, "knowing that anyone other than men who were already criminals were going to take the blame for what we did."

When dinner was over, Tommy stood up. "I think we know what we're going to do," he said. "We just need to come up with some good ideas on how to do it, without any of us being killed, identified, or tied to the bandits getting the gold. I'm going to tell the others what we've come up with and see if they agree; maybe they can even add to the plan."

He found the dining hall empty, so he headed toward the bunkhouse. The large crew it had been built for had dwindled, and now, only seven men were currently living there. Four of the original group had decided they would go home to Kentucky and the others were trying their hand at running their own spreads to seek their fortune.

He called the men over to their card playing table and had them sit down. "We came up with a couple ideas over dinner, and I need to know what you think," he said, and he started talking. The men thought they were good ideas, but none of them had any offhand ideas on how to get the gold into the hands of the bandits without linking themselves to it. "We got two more days before the others are to meet here," Tommy said. "Let me know if you come up with anything. Who knows, maybe we can use parts of everyone's ideas to come up with something that might save us all." The men moved uneasily on their benches. This was clearly a very serious situation.

"Tomorrow," Tommy said, "we should all take three bags of gold out of our boxes and put them in boxes to be used for the gangs. And then we'll go out into the fields and bury the rest of our gold. Find a spot away from anyone else's to bury it and put something in the hole or mark your boxes somehow, so it can be identified as yours. We'll be working in groups to get this done quickly, so everyone's going to know where everyone else's gold is hidden, but I think we can trust each other. I mean, after all, we've all known where all the gold has been for this long." He looked around the room to see how the men were taking in his words before he continued.

"The reason we'll need to be able to identify our own boxes is in case any of us get confused or forgetful. That way, if for some reason we have to go dig them up by ourselves and end up finding the wrong boxes, we'll know to cover them and try a different spot."

The following morning, Tommy, his pa, and Jeb, and the ranch hands put their requested three bags of gold into the boxes intended for the gangs, then went out to the farthest fields with the rest of their gold. Tommy had brought paper and pencil so everyone could make themselves a map of the spot where they'd hidden their stash. They chose hiding places about an acre apart and finished the last holes just as it was getting dark.

"Did anyone come up with any ideas on how to get the gold into the hands of those highway robbers?" Tommy asked the men on the way back to the ranch house. They all shook their heads. He was disappointed but remembered that the other men would be coming over to the ranch the next day, and hopefully, they could help figure out what to do.

Inside the ranch house, the women had dinner ready, and as soon as the men washed up, it was on the table. Terry asked if anyone had seen them in the fields.

"No," Tommy replied, "we didn't see anyone all day, but boy, that ground is getting hard now that the weather is colder. We sure dug a lot of holes—pretty deep ones, too. Did you or Patty come up with any ideas for us?"

"No," Terry said. "But we've been trying. The overall plan is a good one, but just how in heaven's name we're going to do it, we haven't the foggiest idea."

"Well," Tommy said, "the rest of the boys will be here by around noon, I expect, after chores. I think we should make our gathering look like a family get-together, in case one of our neighbors comes over for a visit. I'll get some of the boys in the bunkhouse to help out getting things prepared. In the morning, I think I'll go hunting, and ask some of the boys to go too, so we can have some fresh meat for roasting."

"That sounds like a real good plan," Patty said. "Me and Terry can do some baking and get some side dishes prepared."

"I'd like to go hunting with you. Can I go too?" Jeb asked.

"Sure, you can. Just remember, you have to clean what you kill," Tommy said, smiling at him. He went outside and sat on the porch. As he looked up at the stars, he wondered how much time they really had before the Pinkertons got back to Lawrence.

• • •

Fortunately for the McCoys back at the ranch, the Pinkertons were heading toward them at a much slower pace than they'd taken when trying to catch up with Wiley's group. As the McCoys were getting ready to have their family get-together, the agents were only about halfway back to James's place. This was mainly because at every town along the main road west, they stopped and talked with the sheriff, asking him to send a wire or letter to Brigadier General Thomas Ewing in Lawrence, Kansas if anyone showed up spending fifty-dollar gold pieces. They would be keeping in touch with him on their way back to Lawrence, so if anything turned up along the way, they could check it out. There were still three weeks of traveling to get to Lawrence, maybe more.

• • •

On the morning of meeting day, four of the ranch hands and Tommy and Jeb went hunting. The rest got busy preparing things for the family feast. Jeb shot a nice buck, and the four other men bagged smaller game. When Tommy and Jeb got back, they stopped their horses near the spot that had been set up for cleaning game. "You need to get started skinning and quartering that deer while I put away the horses," Tommy said to Jeb. "We'll decide later how much needs to be cut into steaks and how much put on a roasting spit."

At the dining hall, he found the men cleaning vegetables and preparing basting sauce and basting oil for the meat. One was wiping down the tables and making sure there were enough seats for everyone, with a few extras in case any neighbors came by. It'd been a few months since they'd used all of the space they had in there, since so few men were staying in the bunkhouse now.

When the other hunters returned, they took their kills to the butchering area behind the dining hall where Jeb was working on the deer. When Tommy went to take a look, he saw they'd brought back ten rabbits and five sage hens. They were going to have a lot of food for this hoedown.

Two of the hunters went inside and got themselves a couple of knives and told Tommy that the five of them would knock this out in a jiffy. Seeing he wasn't needed, he decided to go into the house and ask Patty to show him again the information she had about those highway robbers and their locations. She went to her room and got out the notes that she had written down, and he took them to the porch to look them over. When he read that some had last been seen in Missouri and some in Kansas, he realized that many of them were close to the locations of the stockpiles they had raided.

A thought came to him. *What if they loaded four wagons with one box of gold in each and managed to let those highway robbers get their hands on them? It would look like they had been involved in the raids on the stockpiles.* He figured they could let the robbers take a wagon in each area, or even just leave the wagons for them to find. Both ways would work.

This was the risky part: they would have to improvise at each location. They wouldn't be able to plan until after they found the specific places the highwaymen were using as hunting grounds for unlucky travelers. It was pretty unlikely that the bandits knew anything about gold stolen from the illegal stockpiles; at most, they would have only heard rumors from the soldiers the general had sent to try and find a trail. And they would more than likely start spending the coins, leaving a good trail for the Pinkertons to pick up.

For now, that was all he could come up with; he was eager to see if the other men had come up with any ideas.

He went back inside and gave the papers back to Patty. He'd just returned to the porch when he saw a large group of riders. Apparently, the McCoys who lived the farthest distance away had stopped at the houses of the others, so they could all ride in together. They left their horses in the corral then headed to the dining hall and butcher station, shaking hands with everyone and saying hello, surprised to see they were preparing for a big family feast. The group headed to the porch of the ranch house.

Thomas Sr. heard the noise of their arrival and came out of the house and greeted them. A few minutes later, the men at the butchering station finished their work and came to the porch as well, followed soon by the cooks, who had just started the roasting fires and needed to wait before they were able to use them.

"Well," Tommy said, looking over the big group, "it sure is good to see everyone together again." He began telling everyone, once again, about the telegrams from Wiley and James and the situation they were in. The men who'd started their own homesteads weren't happy to hear about the state of affairs. Nobody wanted to have to wait a few years to be able to start building a nice ranch of their own.

"You all have it nice here," one said, "while we live out in shanty shacks. We want to start living a good life too; that's part of why we did those raids." He paused and shook his head. "We've decided that if we can't spend our money here, then we'll have to go somewhere we can. You all can have our places and do with them what you like, but we want to be able to spend our money without worrying about going to jail or getting hung."

Tommy held up his hands. "Hold on a minute," he said. "I've come up with an idea that should, if we can pull it off, get any suspicion off of us. But you're right; you can't stay here and spend your money building you some nice big houses and ranches. You couldn't stay and spend it without spending the money slowly, a little at a time, so that it looks like money you got from your ranch. You can't even melt down the gold and make a mining claim in order to spend it. That would look bad for all of us, since Wiley and James have already done that and turned in big amounts of gold to the bank. But I think my idea will work for everyone, so those who want to leave can spend money when you get where you want to settle, as long as you go far enough away and don't spend any gold coins on your way. That means you'll need to get out of Kansas and stay out of Missouri, Kentucky, and Virginia. Arkansas and Tennessee wouldn't be good places to go either. Maybe by the time you reach your new places, the Pinkertons will have stopped looking for the raiders. If we can get them thinking they're not going to find the rest of the gold, there's a good chance that will happen."

That made the men sit up and take notice. "What have you come up with?" one said, and several others nodded eagerly.

"Well, first," Tommy said, "I'm going to need everyone to pitch in three bags of gold to put my plan into action. Wiley offered to send money, and I'm going to take him up on that offer. When he sends the money I asked for, everyone's going to get three thousand that they can use to spend for traveling someplace new, or to live on if you stay here." Having told the good news, he started telling them of his plan.

"It's going to be a little bit risky for those of us who get those wagons in the hands of the bandits," he said. "I'll need the best shots among you, and it would be better if you're the ones who want to stay here, so those who are leaving can get on their way as soon as possible. I would suggest that you start getting what you're taking with you in your wagons, so as soon as the money gets here, you can hightail it outta here. You'll be a long way from here by the time we get the gold into the hands of those bandits, and hopefully well before the Pinkertons arrive."

His words seemed to please the group intending to leave. "But make sure you let us know where you plan to go," Tommy cautioned, "so we can tell the Pinkertons that you went somewhere else when they ask."

Tommy's stomach was rumbling, and he knew his wasn't the only one. It was time to quit talking for a while and eat, but he had one last thing he had to impart.

"I need to know by morning who's staying and who's leaving," he said, "so I can start planning the details of how we're going to do this." He stood up and added, "in the meantime, let's have us one fine family hoedown. We've got plenty of food, some whiskey and beer, some fiddles, guitars, a couple of harmonicas, and a banjo. We even set up horseshoe-throwing pits. We have a little time to enjoy ourselves together before anything needs to be done. This will be our sendoff hoedown, so let's have some fun."

There were hoots and holler'n' from the men, shouts of, "Where's the beer?" and a debate about who was going to be first at the horseshoes. The cooks left to check on the fires, and the women said there was going to be food in the dining hall to eat in a few minutes to tide everyone over until the meat was ready. Some of the men picked up some instruments and started playing around with them. Quickly, the homestead was alive with activity.

When the meat was done, the group went into the dining hall, which had been set up buffet style. Before anyone started eating, Terry said she wanted to say grace. Closing her eyes, she asked for God to watch over all in the room and gave thanks for letting them all come together as one family once again. She thanked God for the food, the company, and the happiness that they'd had and asked for all to be kept safe and healthy. She finished with, "Please help all of us live the life we've been dreaming about." And when she whispered, "Amen," everyone else did too. Finally, forks met food, and everyone ate till they couldn't eat anymore.

After everyone had their fill and plates were cleared away, they moved some of the tables to the sides of the hall. The men who played instruments made them sing, and those who couldn't started square dancing to the tune the others made. No one cared that there were only two women to dance with because they were just one big family having fun together.

• • •

When some of the McCoys were preparing to head back to their own homesteads the next morning, William Thomas said to Tommy, "We talked everything over last night in the bunkhouse, and we'll get the three bags of gold back to you within two days." Then he told him who among them had decided to leave Kansas. There were three groups going in different directions: William Thomas (Will), William S. (Bill), William I. (Billy), George H (GH), and George (G), were going to California, with a possible stop in Colorado. They said that people were finding gold out there, so no one would be suspicious when they found theirs.

Robesson, with brothers William C. (Willy), and Tom who'd fought together, were setting off for Montana. They'd heard of gold strikes there, and it was a lot closer than California. Festus, Jones (Jonesy), James Sr. (James), and James Jr. (Junior), were going to the Dakotas first, then maybe over to Ohio.

That meant a few of the bunkhouse men were among those planning to leave, and they'd have to go back to the field and dig up their boxes again. It was agreed that all the men would bring their three bags of gold to the ranch in two days and leave as soon as the money came from Wiley.

Only A.C., Oliver, Aron, and Richard would be staying at the ranch, along with Jeb, Tommy, and Thomas Sr.

That left a teenager and six men to carry out Tommy's plan.

Chapter 2

Preparation

When Tommy went to the bunkhouse the next morning, the men were up and having coffee. "We need to find out who's our best shot from long distances," he said, after sharing a cup with them. "We have two Buffalo guns, and all of us have plenty of rifles. Let's grab those two Buffalo guns. Everyone take two of the best of those seven-shot repeater rifles, with a few boxes of shells for each man. We'll go up into the rangeland and set up some targets so we can see which rifles are the best to shoot and who can really hit the far targets. At worst, we'll all get some practice shooting. It's been a while since we've done very much with our guns."

It didn't take them long to get ready. All of the men who were staying on, including Jeb, rode together to the free-range land. Those who were leaving went to dig up their gold. It took a while till they found an open area that had some fairly high hills on each side so they could try shooting uphill and downhill, as well as shoot on the flat. They set targets starting at one hundred yards and as far out as four hundred yards, using both the flat area and up on the hills. After the best shooters had been identified, they would take some practice shots at targets they'd set up on top of the hills, shooting upward from the flat, then head up to the hilltop and shoot downward, and then shoot across the little valley at targets on the other hillside.

Tommy had brought along several cabbages and four boards to put tin cans on. He placed some branches in the ground and set the cabbages on top of them. He intended the cabbages to represent a man's head. A.C. had brought along the spy scope he had from the war so they would be able to tell if the targets had been hit. They had put seven targets at each distance, with two cabbages at each distance of three and four hundred yards. The other targets were broken branches and a couple of old hats. Tommy said he wanted them to take three shots at each distance standing up, without any support for the rifles, and three lying down or kneeling, supporting the rifle however they felt comfortable.

After the first round of shooting, most of them had hit two out of three targets up to one hundred yards. After that distance, only Tommy, A.C., and Oliver hit targets up to two hundred yards. A.C. hit two out of three at three hundred, Tommy hit one, and Oliver hit all three. At four hundred yards, with those seven-shot carbine rifles, no one hit even one target. Then they got out the Buffalo guns. Everyone took turns at four hundred yards, but only Tommy, A.C., and Oliver scored a hit. They moved the cabbages and hats to five hundred yards. They all got two shots at those, and A.C. and Oliver were the only two able to hit the cabbages and hats; they hit both their shots at each target.

Next, they set up closer targets for their pistols, and everyone hit targets out to about forty yards, which was pretty good for those pistols. So Tommy knew then, in close quarters, they would all be fine, but from a long distance, they were going to have to rely on A.C. and Oliver.

Tommy asked them both to go on top of the hill and shoot downhill at some targets he had Jeb place in the little valley between the hills. After, he asked them to shoot targets he had placed toward the top of the hill across the little valley. A.C. and Oliver used the Buffalo gun for those targets because the distance was between four and five hundred yards. Using it, neither one of them missed a shot.

At the end of the day, they mounted up and headed back to the house. Patty was there to greet them, and she had new information to offer. "While I was at work today," she said, "the wire came through from Wiley, and the money is at the bank."

"Wow!" Tommy said. "That was fast!"

The next morning, all the McCoys were gathered at Tommy's ranch once again. Everyone had brought three bags of gold. They put it in a designated hiding place in the barn, inside four of the strongboxes they had kept to the side, just for those bags.

"Wiley has already sent the money I asked for," Tommy told them. "So now, we have to go to town so we can all open up our own bank accounts, and each can deposit their share."

As they rode into town together they drew a lot of attention on the streets, because they looked like a gang. Even Sheriff Banes was wondering what was up as he watched the group of horses parade by his office. He got up from his desk, went outside, and stopped Tommy to ask him if anything had happened.

Tommy laughed. "No, Sheriff, nothin's wrong," he said. "We're here together because something good happened. One of my kinfolk found gold and sent us all some money. We're here for everyone to open up their own bank account so they'll have some place to put it."

The sheriff shook his head. "Well, lucky you. I wish I had some kinfolk who struck it rich and gave me some money."

"Don't we all, Sheriff, don't we all," Tommy said, grinning. "Only he didn't give it to us. It's a loan we're supposed to pay back when we can."

The sheriff smiled back at him. "Okay, I was just curious," he said. "I've never seen all of you come into town at one time before. Glad it was for something good." Finished, he turned and went back up on the boardwalk and into his office, and the McCoys continued down the street to the bank. Tommy went inside first with the wire and arranged everything with the bank manager, and then the men took turns going to the manager's desk to fill out paperwork. After a couple of hours, they all had bank accounts in their own names with three thousand dollars in them.

Outside the bank, when everything was finished, Tommy told the others that he had to buy some supplies and would be in town for a little while longer. So they parted ways, saying their good-byes one last time and wishing each other well. Everyone was a little sad that it might be the last time they would see each other, but they were a little bit happy too, seeing they all had three thousand dollars of their own to spend how they liked.

● ● ●

Patty and Terry and the men staying at the ranch were in no hurry to get home. Patty and Terry wanted to look at some dresses and bonnets at the general store, and the men needed to go to the mercantile and general store to pick up supplies to use on their mission to find the highway robbers. It took them a couple of hours to get everything they could think of that might come in handy. Patty and Terry each bought two new dresses with matching bonnets and some food for the house. The men bought the things they had picked up, and they loaded up the pair of wagons and headed back to the ranch.

On the way, Tommy talked about more details of his plan. "We need to get five wagons ready to travel with an extra horse tied to the back of each," he said. "And put a saddle in each wagon. We're going to all need bedrolls and our campsite equipment—anything you think we might need for the time we'll be gone, and of course anything that you need personally."

A.C. nodded vigorously. "It might be a good idea for us to bring a razor and scissors so we can look more like civilized people and not highwaymen," he told the group, "like Aron and Oliver are startin' to look." None of the men had paid much attention to grooming since they'd finished the raids, but this pair in particular had grown hair and beards of impressive length. "It's for safety too," A.C. said. "Look like a bandit, you might get mistaken for one when shoot'n' starts."

Aron looked offended. "I don't know about that," he said. "We just might be safer this way. Maybe the bandits will think we're one of them and not shoot us."

Tommy had to smile but quickly got back to being serious. "I'll gather up our foodstuffs and a few other things I want to take. By the time we're finished with that, supper should be ready, and we'll talk over more details at the table. We're probably going to be gone a couple of weeks, so try and prepare enough gear."

When they got to the ranch, everyone got busy gathering things for the journey, and the women started making dinner for everyone, as it was already late in the day. They pulled all the wagons over to the ranch house, after loading all of the equipment they took from the barn and the bunkhouse. They unhitched the horses and put them back in the corral, where they gave all of them extra oats.

Tommy directed the loading of the rest of the goods onto the wagons. "We should put a barrel of flour, two sacks of oats, carrots and potatoes, a water barrel, and an ax in each one," he said. "We need to put one strongbox in a crate behind the driver's seat in the back of four of the wagons. Cover the strongbox with straw, make sure the crate has a good lid, and then put something heavy on top of it. We can put in some empty crates to fill up any extra space in the wagons. Then put all our campsite equipment and bedrolls in the wagon that won't carry a strongbox, along with the meat we're taking. Be sure to bring a couple of rifles for each man, with lots of extra bullets for all your guns, and put them in the wagon with our bedrolls and food. Don't forget to cover them all with a tarp." He was quiet for a minute, watching them work. "Oh!" he said. "Don't forget the Buffalo guns. Put them in the wagon with the bedrolls."

By the time they had everything situated, dinner was ready at the house. They put extra chairs and a table in the kitchen for the ranch hands. When they were all seated, Terry said grace. She gave thanks to God for what they had and asked that He watch over them on their journey and keep them safe. As they ate, Tommy started to explain his ideas about getting the gold into the robbers' hands.

"I want to go to the most distant counties first, where those storage sites were," he said, setting down his fork. "We'll find out the roads the gangs used for their robberies. I hope to be able to just leave one of the wagons sitting somewhere and let them find it. I'm not sure how it's all going to work yet, but I expect to be able to figure out the safest and best way to do it once we're there. I know this is going to be risky and tricky to pull off without getting us identified with these wagons. But I think once we get the first wagon delivered, it will buy us a little time. We'll just keep figuring things out as we go."

At these words, Terry gave him a nervous glance, but Tommy didn't seem to notice.

"As you know, the Pinkertons are on their way. I think if we get the first wagon in the hands of a highway gang before they arrive, the gangs will start spending some of that money." There were nods of agreement from around the table. Gold pieces could buy a lot of comfort, as they all knew firsthand.

"That should give the Pinkertons something to do, so they won't come straight to us at the ranch," Tommy continued. "And hopefully, we'll have enough time to get the rest of the wagons to the other highway gangs and get home well before they make it here. It's going to take us four or five days, at least, to get to the place where we'll leave the first one, so we need to leave early tomorrow morning. I want to get out of here at first light."

• • •

They all went to bed right after dinner, and by the time the sun began to push away the night, everyone was ready. All the horses were hitched to the wagons, with an extra horse tied to each wagon's rear. Tommy and Jeb were mounted, and everyone else was driving a wagon.

It was important to not draw attention as they traveled. They must have looked like a bunch of ranch hands bringing supplies back to a ranch, as travelers they passed on the road only said, "Howdy," or nodded and waved while continuing on their way. No one stopped to ask any questions or wanted to chat, and that made them all feel more at ease. They made it to Vernon County, close to the place where they had pulled off the most distant stockpile raid, in just four and a half days. There, they made their camp and Tommy rode ahead to the next town to see if he could find out any information about where gangs had been robbing travelers.

CHAPTER 3

SETTING THE TRAP

The town was small, but the sheriff's office was prominently placed in the middle of its one busy road. Tommy went into the office and found the sheriff carving fishing lures at his desk. Tommy told him he was traveling through with a group and wanted to stay safe. "What's the best road to travel on, and which roads have been hit the most?" he asked. The sheriff leaned back in his chair and shook his head.

"A group of travelers was attacked just two days ago," he said. He told Tommy where their wagons were when it happened. "I couldn't get anyone other than my deputy to go out looking for them," he said, shaking his head again. "People are scared, and there seems to be at least a dozen men in that gang, by the reports I've been getting. I can't very well leave the town without a lawman and going by myself would be suicide."

Tommy nodded politely and said, "Thanks for the information. We'll sure stay clear of those roads, if at all possible." In reality, that was his opposite intention. When he got back to camp, he told everyone what the sheriff had told him. Then he took A.C. and Oliver with him on a ride to scout out the area where the gang had hit a couple of days before.

They had to ride around twelve miles to reach the scene of the robbery. Once there, they followed the road for a few miles. They saw several places along the way that someone might use to hide and then jump out to ambush travelers coming through. A little farther along the road, they found a spot that looked like a few wagons had been turned around. Most of the McCoys were fair to good trackers, and some were excellent. They followed the wagon tracks to a place where they had been brushed out and then looked carefully on both sides of the road for about fifty yards or so until they found a few hoofprints. They followed the hoofprints about a hundred yards to a place where they could tell a wagon had passed through.

A vantage point was needed. They had to be able to watch over the area from a distance and not be seen. They found one on the side of the road less than a quarter of a mile away. A lookout could keep watch in the lone clump of trees on the crest of the hill there. There wasn't much cover between the lookout and the trail, but they would be able to see any riders from far off, and a man could hide in the biggest tree and hide his horse down the other side of the hill.

They headed back to camp to tell the others what they had found, agreeing to send one of them back in the morning to watch the trail. At the camp, they told the others what they intended to do.

"Once we are sure that this is their traveling route," said Tommy, "we'll take a wagon and drop it at the point their trail meets the road. We should disable it somehow, so it looks like we unhitched the horse and rode it to get what we needed to repair the wagon. We can watch from a distance and see who comes by and run off anyone we think is not part of the gang, but if we see anyone who might be one of those robbers, we can let them check out the wagon and see if they'll try to steal it. Hopefully, they will." The men agreed wholeheartedly. They thought it was a fine plan.

"We'll need to leave two men down there to watch, with their rifles and at least one of the Buffalo guns," Tommy continued. "We'll be taking twelve-hour shifts, so it's going to be a long stretch before someone comes and takes over the watch. I don't care how you divide it up between the two of you while you're there, as long as there's at least one pair of eyes watching the trail at all times."

The next morning, before sunup, A.C. and Oliver left to take the watch. At around three in the afternoon, Aron and Richard relieved them. Then, around three a.m., Tommy and Thomas Sr. took the third watch. When Tommy and Thomas arrived, Aron and Richard told them they had seen four riders going onto the trail from the road, riding slow, like they had nothing to do and were just killing time.

In the morning, around seven or eight o'clock, Tommy and his father saw six riders coming down the trail toward the road. Once there, they split into two groups. Three went in one direction and three in the other. Both Tommy and his pa thought they were highwaymen hoping to find someone traveling on the road.

They hadn't seen anything else by the time A.C. and

Oliver showed up to relieve them. During the night, because there was a bright moon lighting the open ground and nothing but pale, dried grass covering the terrain, A.C. was able to see some dark objects moving down the road. As they drew closer, he was able to make out three riders coming onto the trail from the road. Then, just after first light, Oliver saw three more come in from the other direction, but these three were in a hurry and ran their horses.

Shortly afterward, Aron and Richard showed up, and while all four were still there, eight riders came out from the trail and headed down the road away from them. A.C. and Oliver went back to camp to tell the others, while Aron and Richard kept the lookout. Just before noon, they saw six riders coming in with two wagons pulled by running horses; these were the same horses and riders they had seen leaving earlier, and there was an additional horse tied behind each wagon. The wagons and four of the men on horseback kept going down the trail. The two that were to the rear turned back, and the next time they saw them, they were using tree branches to wipe away the wagon tracks. One led the horses down the trail, and the other started wiping out their horse's tracks. They did this for about a hundred yards, then mounted up and rode down the trail.

These actions made the McCoy lookouts sure these men were part of one of the outlaw gangs. They decided that one of them would stay on watch and the other would go back to camp and inform the rest. They drew straws, and A.C. ended up staying on watch while Oliver rode out as fast as he could. When he got there, he told them what they had witnessed. "I doubt they'll be coming out for another day or so," he said. "Maybe we should get over there with a wagon."

Tommy told them to take the bags of oats, the barrel of water, and any tools they wanted to keep out of the wagon and cover it back up. "We'll drive it over there now and make it look like it broke down right in front of the trail they use," he said. "Then we'll watch and make sure they take it."

At the site, A.C. came down to the road and helped Oliver unhitch the horse from the wagon and put a saddle on it, then they took one of the wheels off and braced the axle with rocks to make it look like something had happened to the wheel and someone had taken it off to repair it or get another one. They rolled the wheel off into the brush and made sure it was well hidden. Then they went into the trees to watch and wait.

It wasn't long before two riders came up the trail.

When they saw the wagon, they looked at each other and laughed, and one of them said to the other, "Someone brought us a gift," and they laughed again. They rode to the wagon and looked around the area, then lifted up the tarp. The McCoys had left it stocked with three wooden boxes, sacks of potatoes and carrots, and a crate full of gold coins by the driver's bench. They didn't take time to examine their booty. They just took off fast back down the trail.

About an hour and a half later, three riders and a wagon appeared from the trail. They looked around, decided the coast was clear, and hurried to the wagon. They pulled off the tarp and threw it in their wagon and then quickly took everything it held and put it in their wagon. It took all four of them to get the box that had the gold in it loaded on the other wagon. When they were done, they hightailed it back down the trail, leaving one man to wipe out their tracks.

Satisfied that the right people had taken the coins, the McCoys hurried to the wagon as soon as the last man was gone from sight. They got the wheel out of the brush and put it back on the wagon, hitched up the horse, and took off back to camp as fast as they could go.

When they got there, Tommy was very pleased to learn what had happened. "Now we just need to make sure that they start spending the money," he said. They rode into town and got a hotel room near the saloon. The plan was to stay a while at the hotel, keeping someone in the saloon on watch for anyone spending fifty-dollar gold pieces.

On the third day, three riders came into town and stopped at the saloon. They got a bottle of whiskey and sat down at the card table. A.C. was the one on watch there. He didn't see how they paid for the whiskey, but when they sat at the card table, he saw them set down a couple of stacks of fifty-dollar gold pieces in front of them as a stake. He finished his beer and went back to the hotel.

When he told the others what he had seen at the saloon, all were satisfied that they had done what they had come to do. "Let's get out of town as fast as we can," Thomas Sr. said, "and get to the next place we'll leave a wagon."

They packed up all of their things and started back down the road. On the way, Tommy had an idea. "Why don't we go across into Kansas to leave the next one?" he said to the others. "A couple of those posters said some of the men were last seen nearby over the Kansas state line." And so they turned west on the first main road they came to heading toward Bourbon County, Kansas.

They had followed this road for about ten miles when they came upon two roads heading off the main one. One had a sign that indicated the route to Fort Scott, and the other bore a marker stating that it led to Harding/Little Osage River, which had been named for the town it ran through.

"How about we head toward the Little Osage and stay away from the soldiers?" Tommy said, and there were no dissenters for the plan. When they pulled into the town, they stopped at the sheriff's office and asked which roads were the safest to travel and which were the worst. This sheriff was again quite helpful about telling them where robberies had been taking place. Tommy thanked him, and they headed out, and when they made it to the spot the sheriff had indicated, they decided they repeat what they had just done: find a good place to watch and see what happened on the road.

• • •

As it turned out, the men who had taken the first wagon were a group of fifteen bandits. When they got the stuff to their hideout and found the gold, no one could believe their good fortune. But one robber was suspicious. "Maybe we just took the bait someone left to trap us?" he said. "I think we should make tracks and get as far away from here as possible, as quick as we can."

The others laughed at him, and one man said, "No lawman in his right mind would just leave all this gold out for someone to take. What if he didn't catch the fellas who took it?" He shook his head. "Naw, no self-respecting sheriff would take a chance like that."

"Iff'n it was a trap," another said, "where's the posse that should've been watch'n it? I think it was only one person driving that wagon, try'n to be sneaky and get this gold over to Fort Scott for an escort. Only he hadn't planned on breaking a wheel." They all had a belly laugh at the thought of some rancher in this situation. Overall consensus was that this was a far more likely possibility than a trap. Besides, they were all imagining what they were going to do with their share, and they didn't want to think about anything bad that might come from this windfall. They had finally made a big score, and now they could take off and go wherever they wanted.

Each man ended up with about three-quarters of a bag of gold for himself, and the fifteen men decided to dissolve their gang, since they now each had a small fortune. They separated into several small groups and went in different directions. Most of them were thinking they were going to go home, now that they had money. But some of them wanted to go somewhere and make a fresh start. What they didn't know was that they were all going to have the Pinkerton detectives on their trail in a short while.

• • •

The Pinkertons had been making their way toward Missouri when they got a wire from the general saying the sheriff from Oskaloosa, Missouri, had sent him a message about some men who had come through town spending fifty-dollar gold pieces. The Pinkertons were still in Kentucky but started making their way at a faster pace, now only stopping at the larger towns to ask the sheriff if anyone came in spending fifty-dollar gold pieces and to contact them by letter or telegraph to the general if this happened. By the time the Pinkertons made it across to Missouri, the general had already sent wires to all of the towns a telegraph could reach along the Missouri border asking their sheriffs to notify him if someone came into town spending fifty-dollar gold pieces.

When they stopped in Joplin, Missouri eight days later and contacted the general, they found out that he had been contacted by at least ten different sheriffs about men spending the gold coins. It looked like they had their work cut out for them. There were so many places to check that their leader, Agent Tucker, decided they needed to divide into five groups of two men each in order to trail the coins.

This was approximately ten days after the first wagonload had been taken from the McCoys. This couldn't have worked out better for the McCoys; they had bought themselves a lot more time.

CHAPTER 4

TAKING THE SECOND WAGON

When the McCoys reached the Little Osage River they saw two roads, one on each side of the river. This was the place where the sheriff had said robberies had happened, so they started looking around for a good base camp. They didn't know exactly where any of the robberies had been, only a general sense offered by the sheriff in Harding.

Unfortunately, the sheriff hadn't said which side of the river the robberies had happened on. They would likely need to stay several days to figure things out. They finally found a box canyon with its back end up against some high rocks, just about one hundred feet in elevation, with a sheer drop into the bottom of the canyon. There were a lot of trees at the bottom, and they were thick enough to hide their camp and wagons. The trees were thriving there because a small stream ran by them, probably a finger of the river coming out of the base of the rocks at the end of the canyon.

Their plan for this site would be very risky for the man in the wagon. Tommy had decided that man would be him, since he had gotten everyone into this mess. The plan was to drive the wagon full of bait down the road and have two men stay back, off the side of the road but within the shooting range of their Buffalo rifles, so as to offer some measure of protection for Tommy.

For three days, they rode up and down a fifteen-mile stretch covering both sides of the river and never saw tracks of other wagons, or any indication that other wagons had turned off the main road. On the fourth day, they were about to give up and move to another area, thinking the bandits had moved off after their last robbery, when six men came up on Tommy's wagon.

Two moved to the front of Tommy's horse pulling the wagon and the others around the side of the wagon. Tommy stopped the wagon and said, "Howdy gents, where you headed?"

"Into town," one of them replied.

Tommy followed his question with another one. "Have you seen sign of any bandits on this road?" Before he got an answer, he said, "I've been told I need to be really careful traveling in these parts."

"Yep," said the man who'd answered before, "and you should've taken that advice. Now, what've you got in that there wagon?"

"Just a few supplies for our horses and the farm, why?" Tommy said.

"Well, because it just so happens that we need some supplies for our horses, and you're going to save us a trip to town."

"What?" Tommy said, making his voice sound outraged. "You think you're just going to take my wagon?"

The man gave a mean laugh. "No, I don't think, Mister. I know that's what we're going to do." He patted some dirt from the sleeve of his shirt before continuing.

"The only thing I'm not sure of is what I'm going to do with you." And he pulled a pistol out and pointed it at Tommy.

He was quick on the draw, and Tommy knew that even if he could've drawn faster, the others would've shot him dead before he was able to shoot more than one.

Oliver and A.C. had been watching from a distance, just off the side of the road. They had gotten off of their horses and readied the Buffalo guns when they saw the riders coming, just in case. The moment they saw the riders pull their guns, A.C. said, "I got the one that pulled the first gun. You pick another one and shoot as soon as you get a good bead on him."

It was going to be some long shooting, as they were a good four hundred yards away. A.C. fired first, and less than a second later, Oliver fired as well. The men heard the gunshots and looked up, and when they did, Tommy took advantage of their distraction and jumped off of the side of the wagon, away from the bandits. As he hit the ground, he started hightailing it into the trees. He didn't look back to see what happened, as his only goal was to put distance between him and those pistols. Running as fast as he could through the trees, he zigzagged left and right so that if they did shoot at him, they would likely miss.

The man who had pulled his gun didn't have a chance to even turn and look at Tommy before a fifty caliber slug hit him in the middle of his chest, knocking him off his horse. The man on the horse next to him turned to watch him fall and caught Oliver's bullet between his eyes, darn near taking his head off. The other men's horses spooked, and their riders struggled to get them back in control while simultaneously trying to get a shot off at Tommy. They managed to take a couple of shots in the direction Tommy had gone.

In their panic, some of the men fired their pistols in the direction of A.C. and Oliver, even though there was no way they could come close to hitting them. They turned their attention back to Tommy and started shooting at him through the trees. They each took two or three shots, but trees were all they managed to hit. Realizing that if they were going to get the wagon they had to grab it and run, one of the men jumped straight from his horse onto the wagon seat. He must have done this a few times before, as he managed to do it very smoothly. He grabbed the reins and whipped them so it would take off at a run. The three riders still on their horses grabbed the reins of the riderless horses and took off behind the wagon, leaving the two dead men on the ground. They were out of sight in a few seconds.

A.C. and Oliver got on their horses and rode to where Tommy had run into the trees. They hollered for him to come out, yelling that the gang was gone. In a few minutes, they heard him hollering back. When he reached them, he climbed on the back of Oliver's horse. Back at the camp, Tommy told the others to get things packed up; they had to move out as quickly as they could, because they'd had to kill a couple of the robbers and didn't know how their fellow outlaws would react once the remaining men made it back to their hideout.

It took them over half an hour to get everything loaded and the horses saddled and harnessed to the wagons.

They took off at a fast pace, their destination Linn County, Kansas. It was the closest county to Bates County, Missouri, which was where they had raided a bounty site, and the closest place to their route back home.

CHAPTER 5

THE PINKERTONS FOLLOW THE GOLD

The leader of the Pinkertons, Agent Tucker, had taken a while to decide which of his men were going to work together as partners. Finally, he decided he would be paired with Jasper, Cody with Will, Jim with Thaddeus, Dale with Jared, and Jake with Art. He did his best to combine men who had more experience chasing outlaws with men with less experience, to help the newer men learn—and for their protection.

The Pinkertons had made themselves a map of the towns in Kansas where it had been reported that men were spending gold pieces. There were a couple of reports that the men were still in town, and one such place was close to their current location. The rest of the reported places lined up in a way that, on their map, seemed to indicate the men were headed in a definite direction. Although there was no way for them to know if the men might change paths, the Pinkertons thought it would be best for some of them to go where they still were and for the others to head to the towns that might be their next stop to, hopefully, head them off.

Cody and Will made it to Redfield only to find that the men had left the day before, headed north. There had been three men in that group spending coins, so they set out north, hoping to find the tracks of three riders on the road somewhere ahead.

But the road was full of old and new tracks, and at the end of the first day on the road, the agents were hit by a rainstorm. They figured the storm was going to help them by washing out old tracks, and the three men would now be leaving a fresh trail. It began raining quite hard, so they decided to stop and wait it out. It took several hours for the rain to pass so they could continue.

The next afternoon, they found three sets of fresh tracks on the road to follow. That evening, they came to a small town named Hammond, which had a saloon and a hotel. They went to the sheriff's office and introduced themselves, then asked about three riders coming into town. Sheriff Barnaby told them that three men had ridden in and had gone straight to the saloon, then to the hotel. He thought they had put their horses up at the livery behind the hotel.

Outside the saloon, the Pinkertons pinned their badges onto the insides of their jackets. They decided to go in one at a time, leaving a minute or so between them, so it wouldn't seem like they were together. Cody walked in first, went up to the bar, and ordered a beer. A minute later, Will came in and asked for a bottle of whiskey and a glass, which he took over to an empty table that was close to a card game. At the card table there was a stack of gold coins in front of two men.

Will poured himself a drink and started sipping

slowly, hoping to kill some time so that the third man could be identified.

As Will poured his second drink and Cody was ordering another beer, a man came through the door and walked to the card table. They heard him tell the men behind the gold coins that they should go to the boarding house as there were some "right nice-looking fillies" in that place. He laughed as he sat down.

And just like that, the Pinkertons had all three of the bandits at the card table—in a bad position to draw their guns.

Cody turned nodded at his partner. Will stood up, studying the men and their positions carefully. He walked around their table to a place where he wouldn't be in his partner's line of fire but would also be positioned in a way that the men at the table couldn't get their guns on him before he could shoot at least two of them.

One of the men at the table said, "What're you looking at, Mister?"

"Me?" Will replied. "Nothing really, except those gold coins you've got on the table. Where'd you come by them?"

"Now, that's not none of your business, is it?" the man replied. "If you want one, sit down here and try to win it."

Will shook his head. "I was just curious where they came from, since I've been riding all over Kentucky and Missouri looking for stolen fifty-dollar gold pieces, following reports of men who have been spending them."

The men at the table made a quick glance at each other. All at once, all three went for their guns.

Will was ready for them, and at this range he couldn't miss. Before they could get their guns above the table, he had shot two of them. The third had managed to push his chair back and was on his feet raising his pistol, ready to pull the trigger, when Cody, who was still at the bar, shot him. A look of surprise bloomed across his face as the bullet hit him from the side. He turned to look at who had delivered the fatal shot before dropping dead on the floor.

The Pinkertons flipped open their jackets, showing their badges to the startled men in the bar, and Will said, "Don't worry, folks, we're the law. We've been on the trail of a bunch of outlaws who stole this gold from the northern army. Someone get the sheriff. We'll wait right here."

When the sheriff arrived, he asked if the men at the table had tried to draw first. When this was confirmed by everyone in the saloon, he told the Pinkertons, "I guess you got your men."

"Yeah," answered Cody, "only now we can't find out any more information. We'll need to check them and their hotel room and see if they have any more gold we need to get back."

One of them had his saddlebags with him, draped over his chair. The agents found them filled with his share of the gold. The other two had left their saddlebags hidden under the mattress in the hotel room. The Pinkertons gave the gold to the sheriff and got a receipt for the amount. They asked him to wire the general to tell him what had happened and to keep the gold until one of the general's men came to pick it up.

Mounted up, they headed to Deerfield.

Jim and Thaddeus were there already and had been luckier than Cody and Will. The thieves they were after had been living it up in the boarding house and saloon for the past couple of days and hadn't yet left.

The two Pinkertons introduced themselves to Sheriff Collins, then told him about why they were there. Sheriff Collins knew exactly which men they were looking for. "They're still in town," he said, "although, I don't rightly know exactly where they are just now." Then he asked, "You want me to come along with you to find them?"

Jim and Thaddeus exchanged a glance. "I think we'll be better off if we walk in and they don't know we're with the law," Jim said. "Might give us a better chance to get them alive."

"You're probably right," the sheriff said, "but I'll wait outside, just in case one of them gets a chance to make a break for it." Apparently, nothing very exciting had happened in the town of Deerfield in quite a while.

Jim and Thaddeus decided to check the saloon first. Walking up to the bar, they both ordered a drink so they could take in the surroundings. They quickly noticed a man at the poker table with a few gold coins in front of him. As they approached him, he happened to look up and see their badges, and the man shoved his chair back and jumped up, going for his gun. As soon as he pushed his chair back, the Pinkertons knew what was going to happen, and they were reaching for their own leather before he completely stood up. The man fired wildly and hit the mirror behind the bar, but both the Pinkertons hit their mark, and he fell over on top of the card table. The man's saddlebags were on the floor by his feet. They were full of gold.

The sheriff came in at the sound of gunfire. His eyes went wide when he saw the dead man. "While I was waiting outside, I watched the other two head over to the boarding house," he told the Pinkertons. "I just saw them walk inside."

The sheriff asked a couple of men to help the owner clean up and to get the undertaker, then told the Pinkertons he'd take them to the boarding house.

"I didn't like the looks of those men when they came into town," the sheriff said as they walked. "I had a feeling they were up to no good."

The sheriff stopped in front of the boarding house. "Let me go inside and find out where they are," he said. "I'll come out and let you know. But put your badges where they won't see them. I don't want any innocent people getting hurt because some thief gets nervous." And he went inside to size up the situation.

He wasn't gone more than ten minutes. "They've gone upstairs with a couple of women," he said when he returned. "The owner told me they're in rooms five and six, at the end of the hall." He looked over the Pinkertons' jackets to make sure they'd hidden their badges. "Now, you boys be careful," he said. "Don't let those women get hurt. I'll be outside in case they try to jump out the windows."

Once inside, the owner showed them the rooms. They were side-by-side, so they would have to take them at the same time.

The Pinkertons got in position in front of the doors, and each held out three fingers. Slowly, they began folding in one finger at a time. At the third finger, they both kicked the doors open. In room five, the man was just unbuckling his pants, and the woman was on the other side of the room. Instead of dropping his pants, he went for his gun, and Thaddeus, who had kicked in the door, shot him.

Jim, upon kicking in the door to room six, found his man was sitting on a chair, and the woman was sitting on his lap. When the door came flying open, the woman screamed and jumped to the side of the room by the window. When the man went for his gun, Jim had no choice but to shoot. It was all over before anyone had a chance to say anything; each dead man had their saddlebags full of gold in their rooms.

They counted all of the gold in the sheriff's office, and Sheriff Collins signed a receipt to show the amount that had been turned over to him. "Minus the cost of a new mirror for the saloon," he said, "this is what I'll have for whoever comes to get it."

Pocketing the receipt, Thaddeus said, "Well, Sheriff, we've recovered some of the gold, but we still haven't found out where they got it, or how they found out where to take it from. There's still a bunch running loose that we have to track down, and maybe we'll get some information from one of them." He held out his hand for the sheriff to shake. "Thanks for your help," he said, "and let us know if anyone else comes into town spending more gold coins."

The sheriff nodded. "I suppose one of the general's men will be coming to claim this gold?" he said, probably hoping for more excitement.

"You can bet on that. Don't know how soon, but someone'll be along."

Jim and Thaddeus headed out of town toward El

Dorado Springs, where another report had come from. They were hoping they might catch the bandits on the road or join up with the other Pinkertons along the way.

• • •

The Pinkertons had made a rendezvous plan for seven days from the day they split up. They were to meet at Cedar Springs, in Cedar County, which bordered Vernon County, at El Dorado Springs. The four Pinkertons who had found six of the bandits met up on the road between Deerfield and El Dorado Springs and decided to head together for Cedar Springs.

Meanwhile, the third pair of Pinkertons, Dale and Jared, had made it to their destination, which was the town of Walker. This was the place Agent Tucker thought their bandits were headed to, and he wanted to see if a couple of them could get there before the bandits arrived. When they arrived in Walker they checked in with the sheriff and discovered that the men they were after hadn't arrived. Though there was no guarantee they would show up at all, they decided to wait anyway.

They had been there a day and a half when the group of bandits rode into town and stopped in front of the saloon. To their misfortune, this happened just as the Pinkertons were walking down the boardwalk, coming from eating dinner at their hotel. Stepping up onto the boardwalk, the bandits saw the Pinkertons walking toward them. When one of them saw the Pinkerton badge, he pulled his gun out, yelling, "Pinkertons!" The agency's reputation had apparently grown to the point of reaching the ears of these outlaws.

He fired and missed, hitting a support pole for the

boardwalk roof. Dale and Jared drew their guns fast and fired. They hit the man who had shot at them square in the chest, then dove into the dirt, trying to take cover behind the horses that were tied to the rail. The other two bandits grabbed the reins of their horses and jumped on. They fired again at the Pinkertons, making the dirt fly in front of them. Dale and Jared rolled to their left and came up shooting as the bandits spurred their horses and tried to get away. They'd barely gone ten feet when both were shot out of their saddles.

When the Pinkertons checked the horses, they found the gold. They turned it over to the sheriff. Their job done, they also headed for Cedar Springs.

• • •

Jake and Art were the fourth group of Pinkertons. They were headed to El Dorado Springs trying to head off other bandits when they came upon three riders on the road. When they got within shouting distance, they yelled to the men to hold up, because they wanted to talk to them. But the men didn't give them a chance to get any closer and bolted off into some trees, where they jumped off their horses. They started shooting before Jake and Art actually got close enough to be hit.

Jake and Art each had one of those new seven-shot carbine rifles, and they always carried extra bullets in their pockets. They grabbed their rifles and dismounted, one heading to the right of the shooting and the other to the left.

The Pinkertons stayed out of range of the men's pistols and traded shots for nearly an hour. In the end, they managed to pick them off, one at a time. The robbers made a pretty futile and desperate stand, but they never gave up.

Jake and Art gathered up the robbers' horses and found the gold in their saddlebags, then started toward Cedar Springs to meet with the rest of the Pinkertons.

The last pair of Pinkertons was Agent Tucker and Jasper, one of the newest men on the Pinkerton force. They, too, were trying to head off the gold-spending thieves. They made it to a town named Schell City, which they thought would put them ahead of the robbers. But they were wrong; the robbers had gotten there first. Agent Tucker was perhaps too arrogant for his own good. He had decided he was sure of his quarry's plans and motives. In reality, he didn't know anything about them. He assumed he and Jasper were well ahead of the men and would end up waiting around town for them to arrive. Because of that, he didn't alert the sheriff when they got to town. It had been a long, dusty ride, and they were thirsty, so he decided they would grab a beer in the saloon.

Agent Tucker and Jasper were tying their horses to the railing when the three bandits they were after came out of the saloon. The bandits couldn't hide their shock and surprise at seeing two men with Pinkerton badges on their lapels. Agent Tucker had about a second to realize he had made a mistake before the outlaws drew their guns and fired. Two of the men had aimed at Jasper, hitting him in the shoulder and the leg, but he had managed to get off a shot, killing one of them. Agent Tucker dove under his horse and got a shot off from underneath it, killing another one of them. The desperado still on his feet had a clear shot at Jasper, who was feebly trying to get back on his feet. The man was so close to him he only had to swing his pistol slightly to have the barrel center mass on Jasper, and he pulled the trigger, killing him. Then he ran across the boardwalk to their horses, firing wildly toward where Agent Tucker was hiding.

The bandit got to his horse, turned it around, and mounted. But Agent Tucker had crawled up on the boardwalk and rolled across it to the window alcove of the saloon and was now kneeling there. As the highwayman climbed onto his horse, he turned to fire once more at the place where he thought Agent Tucker still was. He was surprised to hear a shot come from an entirely different direction. The bullet hit him in the ribs and he fell out of the saddle. Agent Tucker ran over to him and kicked away his gun. He rolled the man over and asked, "Where did you get the gold?" The man coughed and a dark crimson stream of blood came out of his lips. He looked into Agent Tucker's eyes and said, "We got it from a wagon we stole," and died.

Tucker left him in the street and ran back to Jasper, only to find him dead, lying facedown in the dirt. The sheriff had come out to the street upon hearing all of the shooting. The agent showed the man his badge and told him he had been following men who were been spending gold coins from a stash that had been taken at the end of the war.

He asked the sheriff if he would take care of the burial of his partner, notify the general about the recovered gold, and send a letter to the Pinkerton Agency about the way his partner had died. "I'll report from Cedar Springs as well," he said, "but you can notify them sooner than me." Feeling anger and blaming himself for not being careful enough to keep them both alive, he got right on his horse and headed away from town, anxious to meet up with the rest of his men and find out if anyone else had gotten hurt or killed in the last few days.

It was five days after being notified by the general about men spending gold coins. Now just nine Pinkertons were headed for Cedar Springs. They would have a lot to talk about.

CHAPTER 6

JOINING THE GANG

The McCoys still had two boxes of gold, but they wanted to get out of Bourbon County, Kansas, as quick as they could, so they headed toward Pleasanton, in Linn County, Kansas. It was the closest place across the border from Bates County, Missouri, where one of the North's army bounty storage sites had been.

When they arrived in Pleasanton, they checked with the sheriff's office to find out which roads were safe and which were not, telling him they were on their way to Lawrence, Kansas. Sheriff Cole, realizing they would have to cross the Sugar River to get to where they were headed, shook his head. "If there's any way you can go some other direction, I would, if I were you," he told them.

The roads near the Sugar River were being hit hard by bandits, he told them, and when they raided travelers, they were not leaving any survivors. But Tommy's men had no other choice of route. "Be real careful when you get near that river," Sheriff Cole said. "Get across it and out of there as quick as you can."

They made camp along the road, well before the river,

so as not to get surprised by the river road bandits. Hoping the bandits hadn't started expanding their pillaging zone, they got very few hours of sleep. The next morning, figuring that they would reach the river before noon, they decided to put two riders in front to keep a lookout, till they found a place to camp. After finding the river, they followed the road alongside of it for a few miles before the two lookout riders spotted a good place to make a camp. They chose a location they could defend, in case anyone tried to rob them before they wanted it to happen.

After getting the horses situated and the campsite set up, their plan was to place a couple of riders a good ways in front of the wagon they wanted stolen. They thought a mile ahead would be about the right distance, so they could let anyone they would meet on the road pass them and have time to double back and come up on them from behind, if needed. They would keep the two Buffalo guns within range, trailing behind their wagon. The plan was to travel the roads that paralleled the river on both sides till someone made an attempt on the wagon. Tommy and Aron were going to be the riders out in front of it. Thomas Senior would be driving the wagon, A.C. and Oliver would be on the Buffalo guns, and Jeb and Richard would stay back at the camp. During the trip to the river, Tommy had come up with a plan and an elaborate story to go along with it.

On the second day they were there, six riders came up on Tommy and Aron. They stopped them and one of them asked, "What're you two boys doin' out here?"

"We just got fired for gettin' in a ruckus over in Hillsdale the other day," Tommy answered. "We were supposed to be guarding my uncle's wagon while he traveled to Fort Scott, where he was supposed to pick up a soldier escort."

"Hmm," one of the men said. "Now, just what does he need a soldier escort for?"

"Well, he's a mean, old, distrustful son of a gun and has some gold he found," Tommy said. "He wants to get it to a bank that he trusts."

"Gold, you say?" the rider replied. "That sounds pretty interesting. Why don't you boys just take it from him?"

Tommy laughed. "Because he knows us; he's our uncle. Iff'n we did, we'd be on the run for the rest of our lives. Even though it would serve him right, we can't do it." He paused, as if thinking. "What about you boys, would you be interested in taking the wagon?" he said. "Thing is, we can't be there to get recognized, but we can show ya where he'll be. Another thing is, ya can't kill him. After all, he is our uncle. We'll show ya where to be and when to be there, for a fair share of what's in the wagon. Whatta ya think?"

The rider was quiet for a minute, and when he finally spoke, he said, "It's not my decision. There's some more of us back at our place, and everyone needs to agree, especially, since we don't know anything about you. If you want to come with us, I can talk about it with everyone and see what happens."

Tommy and Aron looked at each other and nodded. "Sure, why not? Can't hurt to ask." At that, the riders turned and started traveling at a fast pace, with Tommy and Aron following close behind. Tommy and Aron exchanged a glance as they rode along, and Tommy said in a low voice, "Good thing they didn't need to go in the direction we just came from, or we'd have us a real pickle. We'll just have to play it by ear."

After a while, the wagon with Thomas Senior at the reins made it to the place they'd used to turn around each day and head back toward their camp. He was a bit surprised when he didn't see Tommy and Aron on the other side of the river, as expected. Not knowing what to think, he just did what he usually did and turned around, going back toward their campsite on the other side of the river. He hoped the two had just gone on ahead and he'd somehow missed them. When he got back to the camp and found that Tommy and Aron hadn't showed up, he started to get worried.

CHAPTER 7

THE AMBUSH AND GETAWAY

The hideout was a small rundown farmhouse with an aged roof that extended over the rough wooden planks that were the porch. The barn made you think it was a miracle the walls were still able to hold up the roof. Six men came out of the house and stared at them suspiciously, as if wondering what these two were doing there. The one who had talked to Tommy explained the situation to the others, and they talked quietly among themselves. Tommy and Aron couldn't hear what was being said. A couple of minutes passed, and the man they had talked with came back to them. "We'll do it," he told them, "but there had better be a lot of gold in that wagon. Let's just say that if there isn't, you won't need to be looking for a place to live. Now, when is that wagon coming through?"

Tommy smiled. "He should be on the road we were supposed to be taking sometime tomorrow, late afternoon. We'll show you which one. I think I know a good place where it can be done, and we can watch from a distance." Aron nodded, playing along. "We'll need to leave by mid-morning to get there in plenty of time to be ready."

"All right then," the man said. "We'll leave in the morning. You boys can bunk in the barn. There'll be something to eat in a little while. Go make yourselves comfortable."

Tommy nodded, and he and Aron took their horses to the barn and settled their bedrolls on some hay. When he was sure no one else was nearby, Tommy told Aron, "I'm going to sneak out tonight and go back to the camp to tell the others what to expect. I just hope I'll have enough time to get there and back before someone finds out I'm gone."

As the sun was setting, the man who was their contact came into the barn with a couple plates of beef stew. He told them to rinse the plates in the bucket on the porch and leave them there when they were finished. "Be sure and get a good night's sleep," he said. "We'll be leaving before noon to make sure we get to where we need to be in plenty of time."

As soon as the last light went out in the farmhouse, Tommy saddled his horse and walked him quietly out of the barn. He didn't mount up until he was sure they were far enough away that they wouldn't be heard. He took up a fast pace, but not so fast as to burn up his horse. He figured he had almost twenty miles to cover to get to their camp and had to use the same horse for the ride back.

Jeb was on watch. As he saw Tommy approaching, he hollered to the others and they all got out of their bedrolls to find out what had happened.

Tommy filled them in on the situation. Then looking directly at his pa, he said, "You need to be on that side road that's about ten miles downriver, the one that comes over the hill to meet the river road, by around two o'clock. You'll need a horse saddled and ready, trailing the wagon."

He turned to A.C. and Oliver and said, "You need to get there early, set up in the trees, and to be ready to start shooting as soon as they approach Pa's wagon." A.C. and Oliver exchanged a glance. Tommy's tone made it clear that their role would be crucial.

"At the first shot," he said to his pa, "you're to jump off the driver's seat into the back of the wagon, grab your horse, and hightail it out of there. Me and Aron will meet y'all back at the campsite as soon as we can." He stood and settled his hat more firmly on his head. "I have to get back before someone notices I'm gone, or I'm sure they'll kill Aron." With that said, he left.

He made it back to the abandoned farmhouse hideout at about three o'clock in the morning. After unsaddling his horse and rubbing it down as best he could, he climbed back into his bedroll to get a couple of hours sleep, but not before he told Aron what the plan was. After the gang stole the wagon, they would have to come with them back to the farmhouse or risk their suspicion.

The next morning the gang was up and about much earlier than Tommy expected. Everyone in one group, they set out to rob Tommy's father.

• • •

It was around noon when they got to where Tommy said the wagon would be turning off the side road onto the river road.

They pulled the horses into the cover of some trees about a quarter-mile away from that spot. They were far enough away that they were sure they couldn't be seen, but they had a clear view of the side road as it came over a hill and descended to the river. They seemed confident they could mount up and reach the place where the roads joined before the wagon got there. As they all settled in to wait, their contact man said, "You had better be right about all this, Mister. We don't take kindly to somebody wasting our time."

A thick-chested man seemed to be their leader. "When we do this," he said to Tommy, "I'll be staying with you two right here while the others go get the wagon."

"That's fine with us," Tommy said, "as long as you don't kill him or let him see us."

"Well," the leader replied, "if he starts shooting at any of the boys there, I can promise you they'll try to protect themselves, but they'll try not to kill him."

The rest of the McCoys had set out early at the urging of Thomas Sr.. He wanted to make sure they would arrive before Tommy and the gang showed up. Arriving well before midmorning, A.C. and Oliver got into position with the Buffalo guns in a group of trees about three hundred yards away from where the roads met. There, they had clear shooting distance and cover to use in case they were shot at. Thomas Sr. kept the wagon below a rise on the side road, just past the hilltop, where the gang would be able to see him coming down the hill toward the river. They were all hoping the robbers would use the place Tommy said and not choose one of their own somewhere else.

Tommy's father waited till he thought it was around two o'clock in the afternoon and then started driving his wagon slowly down the road. He had cleared the rise and was headed down the hill toward the river when the gang spotted the wagon.

Tommy said, "That's him. Here he comes! Get ready."

The leader looked at Tommy and said, "Kinda strange, him coming down the road all alone with a wagon full of gold."

"Well, we were supposed to be the guards," Tommy said. "Maybe he couldn't find anyone he trusted to come with him to the fort."

That seemed to satisfy the leader well enough. He turned to his men and said, "Well boys, we're here. Go see what he's got in the wagon." But there was something about the way he said it that made Tommy think he didn't believe there would be any gold there.

The men mounted up and started riding slowly toward the side road.

They reached it well before the wagon and stopped there to wait. A.C. and Oliver watched them come out of the trees, stop at the road, while getting into their firing positions. When Thomas Sr. got to the river road, he stopped the wagon where the riders were waiting and said, "Howdy boys, you get a break from working the ranch?"

"Naw," one of the riders said, "this here's a toll road, and we're here to collect the toll."

Thomas Sr. scowled. "I ain't got no money," he said. "Besides, since when does a body have to pay to use a road?"

"Since now," said the outlaw, drawing his gun.

The moment the gun came out, Thomas Sr. stood up, and one right after the other, A.C. and Oliver fired their Buffalo guns, hitting the man with the gun and the closest man to him, knocking them off their horses.

Thomas Sr. jumped over the seat of the wagon into the back, where he grabbed the reins of the horse he had tied behind the wagon. He yanked the reins free and jumped on the horse's back.

When the other gang members witnessed the two men getting shot off their horses, they turned to look at where the shots had come from.

Tommy watched the leader, worried about his reaction. "I guess the guards were staying away from the road," he said.

The men at the wagon started shooting toward the trees, where the shots had come from, as Thomas Sr. spurred his horse. When the men heard the horse gallop off, they turned their attention back to the wagon. Since they weren't supposed to kill the driver anyway, they let him go. One of them jumped on the wagon and started the horse running down the river road toward Tommy and Aron, while the rest of the men kept shooting at the trees till the wagon had gone. Then they turned and ran after it.

When the wagon reached the group, they pulled their horses in behind it and followed it down the road. As they galloped along, the leader told Tommy and Aron they would get back to the farm and divide up whatever was in the wagon. They rode hard for a good ways before they slowed down to give their horses a rest. They traveled the rest of the way to the farm at a pace that would make a person think they were just coming back from an outing to town.

• • •

When the men pulled into their hideout, they stopped the wagon by the porch. The driver, just as curious as everyone else, jumped into the back of the wagon and started opening the crates; of course, two were empty, and one had a bunch of hay inside. The rest of the contents were just a water barrel, some sacks of potatoes, carrots, and oats, along with a couple of bottles of cooking oil and fuel oil, and two barrels of flour. "These crates are empty," he said with disgust. "There's no gold here!"

"There has to be," Tommy said. "It was there when we started out." He climbed onto the wagon and looked in the crates, as if he was trying to find the gold he already knew was under the hay. When he got to the crate with the hay, he started pulling the hay out. After all of it was gone, he turned to the man and said, "There's no gold here, huh? Then what's this in the bottom of the crate?"

The man looked inside, reached down, and tried to pull the box out, but he couldn't lift it. He told Tommy to give him a hand, and they both struggled as they tried to get it over the top of the crate. When they dropped it onto the bed of the wagon, the man took his pistol and shot the lock off of the box, then opened the latch and lifted the top. Inside was a bunch of leather bags with the ends tied closed.

The outlaw grabbed one of the bags, pulled it up, then untied the string and stuck his hand in. When his fingers hit the coins, his face lit with a big smile. "I think we just hit the mother lode," he told everyone, pulling out a fistful of gold coins. "Lookee here, we're rich, fellas! These boys were right!"

All of the men started hootin' and hollerin' and shooting their pistols in the air.

The man who had brought Tommy onto the farm

frowned and waved his arms. "Stop with all that shoot'n you eejits," he hollered. Once the commotion had stopped, he said, "We don't want to be attracting attention. Somebody might come to see what all the shooting is about. Let's get that down out of the wagon and inside the house. We'll count it up in there."

They dragged the box to the edge of the wagon, and two men grabbed each end of it. Everyone followed them inside. They placed it on the table and pulled out all of the sacks, then tossed the box onto the floor.

One of them pulled out a couple of coins to examine them. "These here are fifty-dollar gold pieces," he said with awe. "There's a fortune in just one of these sacks!"

"All right," said the leader, "we'll get this counted up and divided equally twelve ways; since we lost those two, these two newcomers will take their places, so nothin's changed."

As they counted, they made twelve piles of stacked coins on the table. "This gold is going to stay right here till tomorrow morning," the leader said. "Everyone can get their share then and take it and keep it on 'em or hide it, because we can't go spending it around here, not for a while. I'm sure that guy in the wagon is going to go to the sheriff to tell him what was stolen. If we start going into town spending fifty dollar gold pieces, we would be just telling everyone we're the ones who stole it." A few of the men let out groans of disappointment. "Let me think on it some, and maybe I can figger out how we can spend this money without getting caught," the leader continued. "Now, let's get some grub goin'. I don't know about you boys, but I'm starving."

As Tommy and Aron were going toward the barn to

their bedrolls, Aron said, "There's a couple of men talking to the leader in the house right now. I'm going to sneak over by the window and see if I can hear anything." As Tommy continued to the barn, Aron crept to the window on the side of the house.

"Why do we have to share anything with those two?" he heard. "We don't know them, and we don't owe them anything. If they get caught, how do we know they won't tell who we are and where we're at?"

Then he heard another voice. "We should just kill them and bury them out here somewhere, so's we don't have to worry about 'em. Plus that makes more money for the rest of us. Let's just go shoot 'em right now."

And then he heard the leader's voice. "We can do it in the morning," he said. "Let's get 'em to pull some guard duty for us tonight and take care of them tomorrow." That was enough for Aron; he hustled back to the barn to tell Tommy. A couple of minutes later, the leader came out to the barn to talk with them.

"Because of that gold, we're going to have men on guard duty and somebody outside watching the road coming in here," he said. "We're going to take shifts—a couple of hours a piece. You and your partner will be on watch outside on the road from midnight till four a.m." Then he went back to the house.

Aron was worried. "We need to get out of here now, before they change their mind about killing us tomorrow."

But Tommy didn't agree. "Someone would notice us gone too soon, and they'd come after us," he said. "We'll wait to start our turn on guard duty, and we'll have at least four hours before someone knows we're gone."

At midnight, the man who'd been on guard came to the barn and told them it was their turn. Tommy went outside to watch the road, while Aron saddled their horses. When he had all of their stuff ready, he snuck the horses out behind the barn to the edge of the road. They walked the horses a good distance from the farm, then mounted and rode hard and fast toward their camp.

Chapter 8

Turnabout Is Fair Play

They made it to the camp well before daylight and told everyone what had happened. "Those men can identify me and Aron," Tommy said. "We need to go to the sheriff in Pleasanton and tell him our wagon full of supplies was stolen and that we tracked them to their hideout." He paused to wipe the sweat from his face. "We can take him there with a posse, and they'll find the gold, but we'll tell them it wasn't in our wagon. Terry has a cousin down this way somewhere, and we'll tell the sheriff we came here to help kinfolk build a barn and they gave us some supplies to take back with us, and all we want is our horse, supplies, and wagon back."

The men had already packed up and had just been waiting for Tommy and Aron, so they headed toward Pleasanton as fast as they could go.

They made it there before ten a.m. after four hours of riding and went straight to the sheriff and told him what happened. He said, "I told you not to hang around that river. You say you know where their hideout is?"

"Yes, sir, we can show you right where it is," replied Tommy.

"Let me see how many men I can round up for a posse, and we'll see what we can do about your wagon," the sheriff said. "I need to put a stop to all that robbing and killing that's been going on. You boys go over to the hotel and get you something to eat; when I get 'em together, we'll meet you over there."

They had just finished eating when the sheriff rode up with about fifteen men.

"The youngster should stay with your wagons in town," he said. "With you six McCoys and the men I have, that puts us at a little better than two to one odds against those bandits. You lead the way, since you know where they are."

• • •

The gang at the farmhouse realized before daylight that Tommy and Aron had cut out but decided to wait to go after them till it was light enough that they could see to follow their trail, if they could find it. At sunup, they left two men to guard the gold, and the rest took off to find them. They made it to the river road, and since none of them were very good trackers, they weren't sure which way they had gone. They decided they would all go to the place where they had stolen the wagon and split up there—four going up the river road and four down the side road.

They searched till well past midmorning, and finding no sure signs of the men, they decided to just head back to the farmhouse, pack up, and then find a new hideout. The dead gang members were still lying in the road, and as they were about to pass them for the second time, they stopped and dragged them off to the side to hide their bodies. "We don't have time to bury them," the leader said, "but let's at least get them out of sight." By the time they got back to the hideout, it was past midafternoon. The leader told everyone to start getting all of their stuff together. He didn't know just where they were going yet, but they would find some place farther away so they would be safe, in case anyone came looking for them.

It was close to five o'clock when Tommy and the sheriff's posse approached the farm. When they stopped the horses at a distance from it, they could see the men were getting ready to leave. Some were loading a couple of wagons, and all of the others were loading their horses with gear. The sheriff told all of his men to spread out and circle the farmhouse and get as close as they could without being seen, being careful to stay behind good cover. He said to make sure all of them had both their rifles and pistols, as well as extra bullets.

They got into position just as the leader of the gang called everyone to the house. When they were all inside, the sheriff hollered out, "You in the house! You're surrounded, come out with your hands up!"

The men didn't know they were outnumbered two to one and had no intentions of giving up without a fight. One came outside to see if he could figure out who was out there, and the sheriff told him, "Drop your weapon! I'm the sheriff of Pleasanton, and you're all under arrest." That was all it took; the man pulled his gun and fired at the sheriff's hat, half hidden behind a tree trunk, and all hell broke loose.

Someone shot the man, and he staggered backward, then two more bullets hit him, and he bounced off the doorframe and fell to the floor. The others inside started breaking windows and shooting from them. The sheriff's men managed to hit a couple of them as they stuck their heads up to shoot.

The situation was quickly becoming a standoff; the lawmen were getting nowhere and couldn't get any closer to the farmhouse without risking getting killed. Someone ran over to the sheriff and said, "Let's burn them out; if we light the place on fire, they'll have to come out or cook." Tommy heard the man and told the sheriff that there might be something to use as torches in the barn.

The sun was starting its descent toward the hilltops, and they realized when it was dark they would risk losing some of the bandits, or they would risk having some of their men killed as the bandits escaped. The sheriff finally told Tommy to go to the barn and see if he could find something to make some torches they could throw on the house.

In the barn, Tommy and Aron found four old broken lanterns that had some fuel oil still in the bases and some rags, which they tied around some long-handled tools and dead tree branches.. They brought them back to the sheriff.

After dousing all the torches with the fuel oil from the lanterns, the sheriff said, "We'll keep the one lantern that is half-full of fuel. We're going to throw that one at the front door."

As the sheriff passed around the makeshift torches, he told the men, "When I light mine, you all light yours, and then throw your torch onto the house."

He told Tommy to take the cap off the fuel hole of the half-full lantern, light it, and throw it so that it hit the front door. "We'll all start shooting at the windows so they'll stay down. You can throw it then," he said.

Tommy lit the lantern, and when they all started firing, he tossed it against the front door. The lantern's glass broke as it hit and the fuel oil spilled out. Unfortunately, the flame went out as well. With everyone still shooting, the sheriff tossed his torch at the front door to ignite the spilled fuel. The other men tossed their torches on the roof, and a couple managed to throw them through the windows. They stopped shooting and waited.

"You're going to have to come out!" the sheriff called. "The place is on fire. If you come out now with your hands up, you won't get shot." In answer, more shooting came from the house. But the fire was spreading rapidly. As the house began to burn, two men tried to make a break for it but were cut down a few steps from the porch. A couple more got shot at the windows. When the last two inside couldn't breathe anymore, they decided to make a dash out the front door. Their clothes had caught on fire inside. Had they just tried to come out and put out the fire on their bodies, they might have survived. But they came out shooting, and of course, the sheriff's men shot them dead.

The sheriff's men tried throwing buckets of water on the fire but didn't have enough buckets or water. They would have to wait until the fire had burned itself out before going inside to check on how many men were in there.

It started to rain, and most of the sheriff's men went into the barn to sleep. The sheriff kept watch on the front of the house and put a man in the back to watch there as well. The rain helped stop the flames, and when the sun was high enough to see clearly, the sheriff went inside, where he found the rest of the men, either charred beyond recognition or halfway burned and covered in bloodstains from their injuries. The total body count was ten. All of the outlaws had died at that farmhouse. As he looked around, he saw several scorched leather bags on the floor and table, which was also partially burned. Then he saw several gold coins on the floor that had spilled from the bags.

He went back outside and approached Tommy and Aron. "We got here just in time," he said. "These boys were about to hightail it out, and they had a whole passel of gold in that house."

"Gold? They had gold? Then why were they trying to steal our supplies?" Tommy asked, feigning surprise.

"Probably because if they spent any of it, news would get out," the sheriff said. "I got a wire from a general that told me to keep an eye out for men spending gold coins. They needed to get out of the area but didn't have any supplies to get them through to where they were going. You boys can get your wagon and your supplies and whatever else you want that you can find around here and take it with you. They sure won't be needing any of it. I'm going to put these bodies on the wagons they've got here and haul them into town, and then we'll gather up all this gold and take it to my office." What he said next surprised Tommy.

"I'll notify that general about the gold. I'm sure someone will make a claim on it soon enough. I'm sure there'll be a reward for recovering it, and there're probably bounties on some of these men's heads. You say you're from up around Lawrence?"

Tommy thought a second before answering him, then decided, why not? They'd need all the money they could get for a while. "Yeah, about twelve miles outside," he said.

"Okay then, any rewards that come out of this, I'll wire the sheriff in Lawrence, and he can contact you to collect it. In the meantime, have a safe rest of your journey home, and thanks for helping us catch these highwaymen."

They shook hands, and Sheriff Cole went about doing his job while they collected their wagon and the goods it had held. When they were ready to leave, Tommy told the sheriff, "Thanks again for coming to our rescue, and I hope we'll be hearing from you about any rewards." They shook hands again and left.

• • •

They decided a good place to leave the last wagon would be in Cass County, somewhere around Harrisonville. At least, that's what they thought at first. Then a little farther down the road, Tommy told them that he thought he had made a mistake, and they stopped the horses. "I really didn't think it through enough, I guess," he said. "Those Pinkertons are going to find most of this gold. When they add up the amounts they find, they're going to see that it's just a very small amount compared to what was taken." The men looked at each other, unsure how to respond.

"We need to make them think they found a whole bunch of it but aren't able to trace it. I think we need to go home and dig up our gold boxes, empty the boxes, put the gold back into the holes, and then take the boxes with us to the place we leave this last gold. That way, they'll find some of the coins and all of the boxes we have. They won't have any choice but to think that whoever stole it must have left the area with their share."

None of the men wanted to have to go back and dig up their gold and hit the road all over again, especially when they were so close to home. But they decided he was right; the best way to make them think all of the gold was gone was to have them find a lot of the empty boxes. So they started heading toward home, deciding that once they retrieved the empty boxes, they'd head to Paola, Kansas, which was halfway between Lawrence, Kansas, and Harrisonville, Missouri, and leave the last wagon and all the boxes there. They set out for home, knowing they would just have to turn around and make one more trip.

CHAPTER 9

THE OSAGE RIVER BANDITS

When they met at Cedar Springs, the Pinkertons got word from the general that some gold coins had shown up in a few towns around Fort Scott. They headed out the next morning to try and find out where those coins had come from, hoping to find a better trail and more information than they had so far.

It took the Pinkertons two and a half days to draw close to Fort Scott. Gold coins had been spent in Uniontown, Bronson, and Harding, all within a twenty-mile radius of each other. Agent Tucker decided that they would go to Uniontown first, because it lay between the other two towns. Upon arriving, they went right to the sheriff's office and told him who they were and why they were there.

The sheriff told them that they hadn't had any robberies on the roads around them, but there had been some up around the Little Osage River. There had been a couple of men who'd come into town and spent a few fifty dollar gold pieces at the saloon and boardinghouse. They had been in town a couple of days but left a couple days before the Pinkertons arrived. Agent Tucker thanked him for the information and said he was going to leave two of his agents, Cody and Will, in town for a little while to see if those men, or anyone else, returned. The sheriff told them that they were welcome to stay as long as they liked; it was always good to have a little extra law in town.

Agent Tucker decided they would go to Bronson from there and leave Jim and Thaddeus to watch that town. The other five would go to Harding, since it was closer to the Little Osage River, which was the area where the highwaymen had been taking wagons from. They would wait a week if they had to, hoping someone would come into town spending the gold coins. At the end of that week, they would all meet back in Bronson if no one came into town spending the coins. If someone did, they were not to confront them, but stay back and try to follow them to see if they could find a hideout.

"We already know what happens when we go up to them straight away," Agent Tucker said, "Most of these men would rather die than talk." By the end of the day, there were Pinkertons in all three towns.

The Pinkertons were careful not to let anyone but the sheriff know who they were; they kept their badges out of sight and let the townspeople think that they were just saddle tramps needing a rest. About half the week passed before someone came into both Bronson and Harding and spent a couple of gold coins. The sheriff in each town had asked all of the town's merchants and the owners of the saloon and boardinghouse to let him know discreetly and quickly if someone spent any fifty dollar gold pieces. The saloons and the hotels were the first to notify each sheriff.

The Pinkertons went to the places where the coins were spent to get a good look at the men and their horses. Once they did, one of them kept watch on them at all times, waiting for the time they would leave town.

At each town, the outlaws followed a similar pattern; they only stayed two nights and then left, riding slowly, as if they'd had a couple of days off after working on a ranch. Dale and Jared followed the men out of Harding. The other three waited there to see if any more men showed up with gold coins. Thaddeus followed the men who left Bronson, leaving Jim to watch and wait in town.

It wasn't easy for them to trail the men discreetly. In fact, Dale and Jared lost them when they turned off the main road because they had to stay back so far. Sneaking to the top of a rise, the agents from Harding were disappointed to see that the riders had disappeared. There were two small valleys about a mile and a half apart with a hill separating the two. The men coming from Bronson had gone up the valley closest to them, the same place where Thaddeus, also following a good ways back, had lost sight of them. The ones coming from Harding had gone up the valley on their side of the hill that divided the valleys. The agents didn't realize that the two valleys converged.

Fortunately, there was enough daylight left for Dale and Jared to find the trail where the men had left the main road. The agents followed it to the place where the land dipped down into the end of the little valley, which appeared to end at a box canyon. They noticed the side toward the other valley was just a low hill separating the valleys, and they could see a much-used trail winding across it that led to the other valley. They decided to wait and watch to see if their quarry would cross that hill.

Thaddeus lost the trail of the Bronson men as they headed toward the end of the little valley. He also stopped for a while to see if he could get a glimpse of them. Just before dark he saw smoke coming from the end of the valley. He decided that they must've been heading to a campsite or hideout in that area. Being alone, he wanted to be safe, so he decided he would ride into Harding to recruit more help, since it was the closest town and there were more agents there.

Dale and Jared watched the end of the box canyon and hilltop for a while; around sunset, they also saw smoke coming up from around the end of the box canyon. They decided they had found a campsite but didn't want to risk going any closer, so they also headed back to Harding.

They hadn't been there for an hour when Thaddeus rode into town. When they compared information and descriptions of the area, they decided that the men had just left the hideout from two different directions and had returned using separate routes. They decided they would go back in the morning and scout out the area better, and one of them would go fetch the other men from Bronson and Uniontown. They left before sunup the next morning.

When they got to the valley where the hideout was, Dale, Jared, and Jake went down the path they had followed the day before, and Thaddeus took Agent Tucker and Art to the trail he'd discovered. They knew they had to be close to their campsite, so they went in on foot as quietly as they could to see what they were up against. They would meet back at the place where they had split up in two hours.

They found a cabin in the bottom of the box canyon, and they recognized the horses tied in front of it as the mounts the men had ridden. They watched for a while and saw at least eight men going in and out of the building, but they didn't know for sure if any others were inside.

When they met back at the horses and compared notes, they decided to leave four men to watch the place, one on each hillside and one at each place where the riders went off the main road. That way they would know if anyone left and which direction they took. Jake and Art would go to fetch the others in Bronson, figuring that would be safer in case other bandits showed up on the road along the way.

• • •

Inside the cabin, the leader of the gang was fit to be tied when he found out the men had spent some of their coins. "Dammit," he told them, "you boys know I said we can't be spending any of that money around here. Someone's going to be looking for it. We took it not fifteen miles away. Don't you think any lawman will know whoever took that gold is close by? This was a good hideout, but now you've gone and messed that up. We're going to have to leave before someone comes snoopin' about."

One of the men tried to defend their actions by saying, "Come on, we just wanted to go have us a drink and have some fun with the ladies; we haven't had any money to spend in a long time." But his words couldn't fix things.

"Yeah, well that splurge of yours might just end up

getting us all hung," their leader said. "I think we need to split up and get our asses out of here as quick as possible. And whatever you do, don't spend any more coins within a hundred miles of here, unless you don't care whether you go on livin'." He shook his head in disgust. "I wonder just how you made it through the war; you haven't got one brain in your heads between the four of you. I'm gonna get my things together and leave by tomorrow. I want to be able to live long enough to spend this money, so's I can have me a good long life."

Angry and disgruntled about the stupidity of their partners, the others started talking about where they wanted to go and pairing up with those planning to head in the same direction. It wasn't long before they all went to get their stash of gold.

When Agent Tucker saw all of the activity going on, he realized they were getting ready to take off. He wasn't sure what to do, since there were only the two of them watching the cabin, so he circled around, staying out of sight, until he met up with Thaddeus. They decided Tucker would stay and watch, and Thaddeus would go and tell the men watching the roads what seemed to be happening. Then Thaddeus would hightail it to Bronson and try to get the other men back as fast as possible.

After telling Jared and Dale who were watching the road what was happening, Thaddeus took off on a run. He made it to Bronson in about an hour and a half, just shortly after Jake and Art arrived. He told the men what was going on at the cabin and said to wait for him till he got back from Uniontown with Cody and Will, so they could ride back together. He switched to a fresh horse and headed toward Uniontown. He made it there in less than an hour, and switching horses once again, he led Cody and Will back to Bronson.

• • •

At the cabin, the gang leader was making plans for his next move. "If we can make it to the Dakotas," he said to a couple of men, "people have been finding gold up there, so we should be able to come up with a way to keep our gold and live high on the hog for the rest of our lives." Those men thought he was pretty smart and decided they would go with him, figuring that would be their best chance.

When the leader went outside to get a wagon ready, he thought he saw something up in the trees. But he didn't want to let on that he had seen anything, so he continued readying the wagon. When he was done, he went around the backside of the cabin and started hiking up the hill, well away from the area he wanted to investigate. He made it to the crest of the hill, dropped down the other side, and started working his way back toward the spot in question.

As he drew closer, he was moving very slowly, making almost no noise. Unaware he was coming up on the backside of a Pinkerton who was watching the cabin, he crawled over the crest of the hill. Once he got to a spot where he could see the area clearly, he stayed completely still and looked for any kind of movement. He had watched for more than a half an hour when he finally saw movement behind some trees. He looked real hard and made out an irregular silhouette of a man and part of a hat next to a tree. It was clear that the man was there keeping watch on the cabin. He snuck back down the crest of the hill and made his way back to the far side of the cabin.

He went inside and motioned for the two men he was going to leave with to come outside. He told them he needed some help with the wagon. Outside the cabin, he said, "Don't look around. Start helping me put things in the wagon. We're not going to take a wagon; we wouldn't be able to get away. Those tinhorns inside let someone follow them back to the cabin. Just keep helping me and don't act like anything is wrong. We're going to leave on horseback as soon as we can. We need to get the horses on the backside of the cabin, so we can get away without being seen."

"What do you mean?" one of the men asked in confusion.

"Someone's up in the trees watchin' the cabin on the other side," he said.

"Just pack up the stuff you need on your horse. Once we get out of here, we need to ride fast, so act like you're going to water your horse. When you're done with that, take him around the back of the cabin. Don't let on to any of the others that there is anyone out there. The more men that stay here, the longer head start we get." And then he spat onto the ground. "Serves them right," he said, "because they brought this on us. We'll meet behind the cabin and leave together. I don't know how long they've been watching, but I'm sure they sent for help."

The men did as they were told, while the four bandits inside the cabin were trying to play down their idiotic behavior that had put them all in danger.

"It'll probably be at least a week before someone even leaves town to look around, and I doubt that anyone even will," they heard one of the men say.

When the leader and his two partners were ready, they met at the cabin's rear, as planned. The leader told the others to be as quiet as possible till they were well away from the cabin. They sneaked off, leading their horses out of sight of the man watching the cabin. Once they'd crested the hill, they mounted up and started out cross-country, staying well away from any roads.

About an hour later, the men inside the cabin began wondering where the other three were. A couple of them went outside and found that the wagon they had loaded was still there, but their horses were gone. When they went back inside and told the others, some of them wondered if they had gotten out of there that quickly and stealthily, then maybe they should as well. The four who had gotten the rest into trouble said they weren't worried about anything and were going to stay right where they were. But three of the others decided they were going to leave right away. They got their horses ready and started out down the valley on the far side of the cabin.

Agent Tucker saw them leave but couldn't do anything to stop them; he had to stay and see what the others were going to do. The three headed down the trail through the valley toward the road that led to Bronson. When Jared, who was watching that road, saw them, he smiled to himself. *You boys are going to walk right into a heap of trouble*, he thought. But he stayed where he was. He wanted to see if any others emerged from the trail.

Thaddeus, Cody, and Will, riding hard from Uniontown, made it back to Bronson a little over two hours after Thaddeus had left to fetch them. They met up with Jim, Jake, and Art. After getting fresh horses from the sheriff, all six of them headed down the road toward the valley that would lead them to the cabin. About half an hour later, they saw three riders coming toward them on the road. As they got closer, Thaddeus recognized one of the horses from the cabin and told the others.

They all unstrapped pistols, and a couple of them pulled rifles from their scabbards and held them across their saddles.

When the three bandits saw the six riders coming toward them pull their rifles out, they looked at each other grimly. "Looks like the boss was right," one said. "They got somebody comin' after us. Let's split up. Everyone take a different direction and run like hell. If you get caught, don't say nothing about nothing. Let's go!" And they kicked their horses and took off, one plunging into the brush on one side of the road and one turning off toward the other side, the third heading back the way they had come.

The Pinkertons started after them, Cody and Will going after the man who had turned around on the road. The man who had fled to the right of the road had to run uphill, so he wasn't making good time. Thaddeus stopped his horse and took a shot with his rifle, hoping only to wound the man. But, he didn't hit the man where he wanted; instead, he got him square between the shoulder blades, severing his spinal column.

The one going downhill was galloping so fast his horse stumbled and fell. When the man fell on the ground, he hit a rock with his head, which crushed the side of it and broke his neck. As for the one who turned around, his horse was eating up distance as fast as it could. He turned in the saddle and fired his pistol at his pursuers, and they returned fire and kept coming. When the road made a turn, he kept going straight, hoping he would make it into the trees. Cody hooked his reins around his saddle horn with one hand and brought his rifle up with the other. Just before the man reached the trees, he was knocked out of his saddle by a gunshot that grazed his side. He hit the ground and rolled but came up on one knee with his pistol in hand and started shooting. The Pinkertons fired back instinctively; both Will and Cody hit the man, killing him.

They rounded up the men's horses and tied the men's bodies across their saddles. The gold was in their saddlebags. They decided to send Jim back to Bronson with the three dead men to turn them and the gold over to the sheriff. He was to return to the cabin as quickly as he could. The other five started back toward the cabin, hoping the rest of the gang was still there and the other Pinkertons hadn't been discovered or killed.

By the time the reinforcements made it to Jared, who was still positioned on the road to Bronson, the group of bandits who had left undetected had a good four to five hour head start, and the Pinkertons still weren't aware that they had left. Jared and Will were told to keep watch at the road, with instructions to wait an hour, then start working their way toward the cabin till they got within sight of it. One of them was to get to Agent Tucker and find out the plan to capture the rest of the gang.

Thaddeus and the other three Pinkertons picked up Dale, the road lookout on the other valley, and headed toward the cabin. When they got to the place where they had left the horses before, they dismounted and worked their way to the place where Agent Tucker was watching the cabin. Tucker told them of the three who had left, and Thaddeus nodded and said, "Yeah, we got them. But they're all dead."

Tucker swore. "We need to try to take these boys alive somehow," he said. "Let's try to surround the cabin as soon as those other two make it here."

Thaddeus told him, "They're supposed to meet me at the horses in a few minutes. I'll get back over there and wait." The men spread out, making a wide circle around the cabin. When Thaddeus returned with the other agents, Agent Tucker told them all to join the circle around the cabin.

"What will you do then?" Thaddeus asked.

"I'm going try to talk them out," he said.

Soon everyone was in position. "You in the cabin," Tucker yelled. "We've got the place completely surrounded. Come out with your hands up, and you won't get shot." There was a commotion in the cabin, and they could see men crowding around the windows. "Come out with your hands up," Tucker said again. "You haven't got a chance."

One of the men inside told the others, "My horse is right out front. You boys start firing, and I'll try to make a break for it. If I can get past them, I'll start trying to get them from behind."

"That's crazy," came a reply.

"Well, we can't just stay here. We have to try something."

He went to the door and shouted, "Now!" And they broke the cabin's windows and opened fire on the Pinkertons. The man stayed low, trying to hide behind his horse, but a bullet hit his mount, and it went down, leaving him completely exposed. He had bullets in him from four Pinkertons in less than two seconds.

One of the three left inside said, "Let's go out together. We can shoot a hole through the line of men out there and make a break for it. If they take us in, they're going to hang us anyway." They only got about four steps off the porch and were cut down.

The Pinkertons stopped firing and waited, thinking there should have been at least one more man still in the cabin. Finally, one yelled, "Anyone still inside come out with your hands up!" When no answer came, Dale ran to the cabin and snuck up to the door. He jumped inside, his pistol leading the way. Looking around nervously for any motion, he discovered that the place was empty. He went back outside and shouted, "There's no one else in here!"

They knew there had been at least eight men in that cabin when they'd sent Thaddeus to get the others. "Okay," Agent Tucker said, "let's spread out and try to find this guy; he must be hiding somewhere." They spread out and started looking around. Then Jim arrived from Bronson. "Dang it, I missed all the fun," he said.

A few minutes later, Cody hollered from behind the cabin, "I think I found something." When the men reached him, Cody pointed to the ground and said, "Looks like there were three horses here, and they headed up the hill behind the cabin. There must've been ten men instead of eight."

"Huh," Tucker said. "Well, we don't know how long a head start they have, so let's get these men and the gold over to Harding. Then some of us can come back tomorrow and see if we can pick up a trail."

• • •

They turned the bodies and the gold over to Harding's sheriff. Agent Tucker sent a wire to the general and wrote a letter to the agency about the man he'd lost and what they'd accomplished so far. Then, because they had all been on the road for a few days and needed a good night's sleep, he went to the hotel and got rooms for everyone, as well as something to eat. The next morning, a wire came back from the general. It said that a sheriff in Pleasanton, Kansas, had taken out a gang of robbers and found more gold. He wanted them to talk to the sheriff and find out what had happened there.

Tucker told the others that he and Jim would go to Pleasanton. The rest of them were to go back and try to pick up the trail of those three who had gotten away from the cabin. With a couple of good meals and a good night's rest, the men were feeling refreshed and ready to head back out to do their jobs. Tucker told them to meet with him in three days in Pleasanton, Kansas, unless they were able to pick up a trail on those three escapees; if they did, they were to send someone to let him know they were following a trail. Refreshed, seven men went back to the cabin, and Tucker and Jim headed to Pleasanton.

At the cabin, the men followed the trail up the hill to a place where they could see the bandits had struck out cross-country. They spread out and started tracking. They followed the tracks for six or seven miles, until the tracks made a turn and started heading northeast. They followed this trail another five miles to the place where it joined a road. They took the road through several small towns, asking the sheriff in each one for information, but no one had information about three men coming through. They kept going through Prairie City and headed over to Rockville.

In Rockville, the sheriff didn't have any news for them either, but the general store owner told them that three strange men had come in and bought shells for their rifles. He couldn't tell them where they went from there. They decided they would head north, because if the thieves headed east, it would mean they were going to have to cross a couple of large bodies of water or take a long detour around them, including lots of detours to get past the waters of the Ozarks. Going north, they would have to travel about thirty miles to be clear of the water obstacles, but from there, the bandits could go any direction they wanted.

From there, the Pinkertons went past Montrose and on to Clinton, Missouri.

Clinton was a large town, and it took them a good part of the day to check with all of the places the men might have stopped. Most of the business owners said a lot of people they didn't know had been coming in recently, but they didn't remember any three men who particularly stuck out in their minds or spent gold pieces.

There was one day left before all the Pinkertons were supposed to meet up, so they decided they had come to a dead end and would head to Pleasanton, where they could wait to hear any news about men spending gold coins with the rest of the agents.

Agent Tucker had arrived in Pleasanton first and gotten the news about what happened. He told the others when they showed up about the gang the sheriff had wiped out and how the sheriff had been helped by the McCoys.

"Since we're probably about three day's easy ride from Lawrence," he told his men, "we should go pay a visit to the McCoys. After all, that's where we were headed when we turned around in Kentucky. We'll wait another day here and see if we hear any news about those three who got away or about anyone else spending gold coins."

CHAPTER 10

GETTING THE STRONGBOXES

Tommy and his group had headed straight for the ranch and wasted no time in getting there. The McCoys didn't know the Pinkertons were in Pleasanton when they arrived at the ranch, but they felt a strong need to get things done. They pulled up to the ranch house early in the morning, and Terry and Patty came out to greet them.

Terry had suffered during Tommy's time away. She was surprised by how upset she had been at his departure and how she just couldn't seem to stop worrying about his safety and that of his crew. As Tommy climbed off of the wagon, she grabbed him by the shoulders and hugged him. "I was so worried about all of you," she said, "but I was really scared that I would never see you again."

Tommy blushed a little bit, surprised and delighted that he had provoked some real emotion from her. He felt hope rising in him that once again he'd be able to win her heart completely.

He hated that he had tell her they needed to take one more trip and decided that news could wait. So he hugged her back, and she pulled away, reached up, pulled his face to hers, and gave him the first kiss he had received from her in years that lasted longer than half a second. She had tears running down her face and wiped at them as if embarrassed in front of the other men, but she just couldn't help herself. She took his hand and brought him inside the house.

Everyone stayed outside the house for a while, thinking they should give them at least a few minutes alone. When Terry closed the door, she grabbed him again; this time the kiss was a passionate one, and he felt all the longing he had stored up inside him emerging. He kissed her back, offering her all and more of what she was giving him. For so long, they had both been holding their feelings back, each for their own reasons, but now the restraining wall was broken and their feelings were coming out like a great flood.

She had to break off their kiss, even though she felt like she was going to explode inside. All she wanted was to just take him into the bedroom. But she couldn't do that now, not with everyone right outside.

As she pulled away from him, they were both were breathing heavily. "I'm sorry," she said. "I think we're getting too carried away. The others will be wanting to come inside. I bet everyone is hungry." And she smiled at him. "We'll have time for that later when this is over; then we can take up where we left off."

She headed into the kitchen and left him standing there shocked and bewildered. His head was spinning, and he was feeling so good inside that he wanted to just shout out how much he loved her and how happy she'd just made him feel.

Instead, he turned to the front door and opened it.

The others were milling around outside, waiting. As he stepped onto the porch, everyone was smiling and grinning at him. He looked back at them with the biggest smile his face would give him. He started to say something but couldn't get any words to come out, so he began to walk to the wagon. When he reached it, he wasn't sure why he was there and started toward the well. Halfway to the well, he took off his hat and threw it as high as he could, yelling, "Yeeeeehaaaw!"

Everyone started laughing. The relationship between Tommy and Terry had been strained for so long that seeing him feeling so good made them all feel really good too.

Thomas Sr. told the men to take the wagons to the barn. "We'll change horses and go to the fields to uncover those boxes after we've had something to eat," he said.

Patty went inside to help Terry, and Jeb followed. He started to tell them all about their adventure, and being young, he didn't think about not telling them about some of the danger they'd been in. In truth, he was proud to have been a part of it. He wanted to tell everything all at once, and they had to tell him twice to slow down and start at the beginning.

So he started over and told them everything that had happened to him, as well as details of situations he hadn't seen himself. Of course, he made it sound like they were all heroes and should be given medals.

Terry and Patty tried to hide their emotions as he talked about the danger the men had been through; they realized he thought it was a great adventure but were terrified by how close they had come to losing their family.

When Jeb told them they had to make one more trip with all of the empty strongboxes, the women exchanged worried expressions.

Thomas walked over to Tommy, who was standing at the well. He couldn't help but put his arm around his shoulder. "Looks like she's starting to come around after all," he said.

Tommy looked up and his eyes started to moisten. His mouth trembled as he said, "I can't tell you what I'm feeling inside." But then he tried to anyway. "It's like this huge weight has been taken away and a new light has turned on inside me. I hope it never changes. I know I'm going to do my best to keep that light shining. I hope that she feels the light too and that it just keeps getting brighter for her."

"Well," his pa said, "just keep doing what you've been doing, because it's the right thing. It's what she's needed to feel right with you again." He clapped his son on the back. "Let's go sit on the porch and take in some of this nice sunshine, and you can keep basking in those feelings. Enjoy it as long as you can." Thomas felt really happy for his son and was proud of him for taking the time and patience that was needed to break down the wall of hurt Terry felt. It made him feel good that they were really coming together again as a family.

After they'd been sitting on the porch for a little while, Terry came outside and said that breakfast was ready. Once everyone was seated, Terry folded her hands and bowed her head. Tommy felt his breath catch as he waited to hear what she would say. "I want to thank the Lord for all we are about to receive and to thank him for bringing me back to my man and for bringing him back to me. Please, let them all come back safely from this last trip they have to make. Please, let this be the last time we ever have to do anything like this again and let us live a good and peaceful life from here on out. Amen."

Tommy looked up at her when she said the part about this last trip, thankful someone else had told her. He was glad that she understood why they had to make one more trip.

She didn't look at him while she was saying her prayer, but she could feel his eyes on her.

When she finished, she looked up at him, and her eyes revealed the love and understanding she felt. She knew that he didn't want to leave again but that it was something that had to be done if they were going to be able to have a good life together.

The one thing she tried not to show him was how scared she was for him.

After breakfast, the men went to the barn and loaded all of their shovels and picks into two wagons. Tommy and his father would drive the wagons out to the fields and dig up their boxes. The men would ride their horses to the buried gold. Each had a clear memory of the spot where they'd buried their boxes, and once uncovered, they quickly emptied them and put the bags of gold back in the holes, along with their personal markers. When they were finished, they waved their hats, signaling to Tommy and his father that the boxes were ready to be picked up.

Each wagon held fifteen empty boxes. There was one box of gold leftover from their first trip, and back at the barn, they placed half its contents in another box, then stashed the boxes behind the seats of the wagons and covered them with tarps, so they would be ready to leave in the morning.

That night, Terry told Tommy that her cousin had written her to see how she was faring during Tommy's absence, because she'd written her about his return from the war and about her troubled feelings. It was the very same cousin who lived near Pleasanton, the one who'd written her previously and said she was in the process of building a large barn. The barn Tommy had told Agent Tucker they were helping build. He'd nearly forgotten all about that detail that needed reinforced.

Tommy asked Terry to send a letter the next day to her cousin and advise her to tell anyone who might come asking that they had been to her place and helped build the barn last week. He told her to make sure the letter got out on the next stage headed toward Pleasanton, and she promised she would.

The women had drawn hot baths for Tommy, his father, and Jeb. After bathing, the road-weary men went to bed. Terry told Tommy not to worry about setting up his cot by the fireplace because he deserved a nice bed to sleep in. After cleaning up the dishes and pots from dinner, Terry and Patty went to their rooms as well. Tommy was asleep when Terry crawled in beside him. She snuggled up as close as she could, put her arms around him, and put her feet on his. She held him like that until she fell asleep, feeling warm and content that he was in her arms again.

The next morning everyone was awake at sunup. The men got the horses and wagons ready, and the women made them a breakfast of hotcakes and eggs. After one last cup of coffee, they went outside to the wagons and their horses. Tommy was last to leave the table, and as he was getting up, Terry went to him, put her arms around his neck, and gave him a long, loving kiss. As she dropped back from her toes she said, "Please be very careful. I don't want to lose you again."

He gave her a loving smile. "I'll do everything I can to not take any unnecessary risks. I have always loved you; I've just been waiting for you to be able to let yourself feel for me again. Now that those feelings are returning, I don't want to miss them. I'll be back as soon as we get this done." He kissed her once more, grabbed his rifle and hat, and went to the front door.

He didn't see the tears that had started to roll down her cheeks, her heart overflowing. She wiped them away quickly, so if he turned around, he wouldn't see them. He did turn back to her when he got to the door, then he smiled and said, "We'll be back soon honey. Don't worry."

After he left, she wrote the letter to her cousin telling her what she needed her to say. Because they were close and looked out for family, Terry knew she would do what she asked. She told them she was sending a gift by wire for the favor and would need to check with the telegraph office when she got the letter. There would be a bank communication notice, confirming a draft in her cousin's name to take to the bank. She went to town and mailed the letter, then to the bank and arranged for a thousand dollar draft to be sent via telegram to her cousin.

CHAPTER 11

THE LAST DECOY

Tommy and his group had a little over forty miles to travel to get to Paola. They made it there late in the afternoon the following day, sleeping by the wagons just off the road for the night. Once there, they went to the sheriff's office, and Tommy asked him for the safest routes to travel on their way back to Lawrence. He was trying to make him think they had been coming from Pleasanton. The sheriff said that the only trouble he had heard about was up around Hillsdale; everyone traveling on the east side of Hillsdale Lake had been getting robbed, but there had been no reports of anything happening between the lake and Lawrence. Tommy thanked him for the information, and the sheriff walked him out of his office. Nodding at the two wagons, five other men, and the boy, he said, "Y'all be careful. Just stay to the west of Hillsdale Lake and you should be fine."

It was just getting dark when they came to a fork in the road that indicated the town of Hillsdale and Kansas City, Missouri in one direction and Lawrence, Kansas in the other. They took the fork toward Hillsdale. When they crossed a small stream they figured came from the lake, they decided to make camp.

The next morning, Tommy rode into Hillsdale and asked the sheriff which areas travelers had been robbed in. As he told him the current trouble spot, Tommy realized he was describing the place where they had camped. He thanked him and quickly headed back, hoping nothing had happened there while he was gone.

At the campsite, he told the men what the sheriff had said, and they decided they would keep their camp where it was and take the horses and hide them somewhere they would have grass to eat. That way, they'd keep the campsite clear of people but leave the wagons. They kept lookouts far enough away in the trees to be safe while still being able to see anyone who came there.

The next morning, Tommy, Jeb, and Thomas Sr. decided to take a ride to see the lake while they were waiting. The other four were going to take turns watching the campsite. They had positioned themselves on both sides of the area where they left the wagons, so they could see anyone coming down the road toward their camp.

Tommy, Jeb, and Thomas Sr. made it to the lake in less than an hour and decided to try some fishing. Jeb had bought some fishing line and hooks in Paola when he heard the sheriff talk about Hillsdale Lake. They cut some branches and made fishing poles, tied the line to them, and went about searching for something to use as bait. They caught some grasshoppers, dug up worms, and settled in to fish. It didn't take long before they all started catching some. They caught several trout and a couple of catfish before noon, and when they decided they had enough for dinner, they headed back toward their camp.

That night at the campsite, while they were eating the fish they had caught, Tommy came up with the idea to make the wagons look like they were hidden, but not hidden well, so that if someone came by, they could still see them. "This way, no one has to be at this campsite," he said. "We'll make our camp closer to the lake, and someone coming in will think we left the wagons hidden here without a guard. That way, we don't risk anyone getting shot. We can watch from our lookout points to see who comes in, and we'll be able to see if they look like the men we want to take the wagons." They decided that they would all sleep up past the lookout points and leave the harnesses on the wagons to make it even easier for any bandits.

The next morning, A.C., Oliver, and Richard took the fishing poles and set out for the lake. An hour or so after they had gone, five riders came down the road. They seemed to be following the wagon tracks. When they saw the place where the tracks went off the road, they stopped, looked around, and headed down the trail the wagons had taken. When they got close enough to see the campsite, two of them got off of their horses. They quickly spotted the wagons and went back and talked to the other riders. Then all of them got off their horses and walked into the campsite, where they hollered, "Is anyone here? If you're hiding, you can come out. We don't mean you any harm."

After a few minutes, they decided either there was no one around or that they weren't coming out of hiding and started taking off the branches that had been used to cover the wagons. When they lifted up the tarps and saw the strongboxes, they knew exactly what they were and looked at each other as if they couldn't believe their good fortune.

The man that seemed like he was running things said, "Let's get these wagons and get out of here. Clay, you and Russ take the saddles off of your horses and throw them in the back of the wagons. The rest of us will hitch up the horses."

They were quick about getting it done; in just a few minutes they were driving off in the wagons. Tommy and the others who were watching were satisfied that they had to be robbers who were working the area.

When they were gone, Tommy and the rest of the group got the horses and headed to the lake to find the other three who were fishing. They weren't very hard to find. When Tommy told them what had happened, everyone was relieved to have finally gotten rid of the rest of the boxes. "Since we're finished," Tommy said, "let's enjoy the rest of the morning fishing."

Chapter 12

The Three Who Got Away

The Pinkertons were in Paola the night before the last wagons were taken. They'd gotten a wire from the general at eight a.m., saying that three men were in Hillsdale and had spent a fifty dollar gold piece, so they headed toward Hillsdale as fast as their tired horses could carry them.

• • •

At the lake, the men had only caught a few fish. By noon, Tommy and a couple of the others said they wanted to try for catfish at night because that was when the bigger ones come out to feed. "We're done," Tommy said, "and we deserve a day off to relax and have fun." They decided to make a camp right there on the lakeshore. They cooked the fish they had caught for lunch and made a big fire pit, so they could use the light from the fire to fish that night. The McCoys had no idea that the Pinkertons were slightly more than an hour away from the place they had hid the wagons.

• • •

As the thieves drove the wagons down the road as fast as they could go, trying to put as much distance between them and where they took them as quick as they could, the three on horseback got well ahead of the wagons. When they reached the turnoff to their hideout, the Pinkertons were just coming over a rise and saw three riders running fast and then heading down a side road. The riders had already made the turn when the Pinkertons cleared the rise and didn't see them. The Pinkertons sure noticed them, however, as three riders was exactly what they were looking for.

They slowed their horses and moved them into the cover of some woods. They watched the riders to see how far the men were going to go off the road.

When the men rode out of sight, the Pinkertons decided to start heading after them, but then they saw two wagons approaching, and they, too, turned down the same trail. The Pinkertons thought they had accidentally come upon a highway gang making a getaway with stolen goods, so they decided they would check it out. They didn't know if those three riders were the ones they were after, but they considered it possible that they had picked up two other men and made another robbery. They waited till the wagons went out of sight and then hurried to the place they had left the road, following slowly so they wouldn't be seen.

The bandits' hideout was about a mile and a half down the trail. Stopping the wagons in the barn area, they ripped off the tarps and started pulling out the boxes. The first box was empty. The second was as well. As they started opening the boxes and throwing them on the ground, they were cussing and complaining about how they had just stolen a bunch of empty strongboxes. As they came to the last boxes in each wagon, it was obvious that they were extremely heavy compared to the others. Both boxes were opened at the same time, and one of the men hollered, "This one here's not empty! Look what we got!"

"Neither is mine," said the other man. "Take a look!"

"Let's get them in the cabin and take a gander at what we got," one of them said, and they heaved the boxes out of the wagon. They set them on the floor of the cabin, opened them and one of them grabbed a bag and untied it, then stuck his hand inside and pulled out a fistful of coins. "We did it," he hollered, "we hit a big one! These here are fifty dollar gold pieces; there's a fortune in just one of these bags." Together, the men began dumping out the coins and stacking them on the table they used for eating and card playing.

There were fourteen bags in all and fifteen thousand in each bag. They each got two bags and took three thousand from each of the remaining four and made a pile, thus splitting the last four evenly. The man who had gotten the pile of coins started stuffing his pockets as the others put the bags in their saddlebags. A couple of the men slung their saddlebags over their shoulders and one of them said, "I think it's time for us to move on."

"Yeah, it's time we get outta Dodge before someone tracks those wagons here," another agreed.

"Let's skedaddle," a third chimed in.

"Don't go back out the way we came," one said. "There may be someone coming in. We weren't careful about watching for anyone following us."

Three of them went outside and threw their

saddlebags on their horses and mounted up. They took off in the opposite direction from where they had come in. The other two came out right behind them and went to the barn, unhitched their horses from the wagons, and threw their saddles on them. Then they headed off to the right of where the others had gone. They were gone twenty minutes after reaching their hideout.

The Pinkertons had dismounted less than half a mile off of the road and started walking their horses so they could make a quiet entrance. By the time they made it to the cabin and barn, the bandits had been gone for about twenty minutes. The front door of the cabin was open. No one was on the property, not even a horse. After yelling for anyone inside to come out with their hands up and getting no answer, they came through the door. They found the two strongboxes on the floor, empty. When a couple of men checked out the barn, they saw the pile of boxes laying on the ground next to it.

"How could they have known we were coming?" one of them said. "I know they didn't see us."

"It doesn't matter now," said Tucker. "Let's look around and see if we can find fresh tracks." They looked all around, but the multitude of fresh tracks were confusing, and they couldn't tell which direction they had gone. "I wonder what they've done with all that gold," said Tucker. "I bet they hid it somewhere and took the stuff they got from the wagons to supply them to get away."

They could tell that the strongboxes hadn't been on the ground for very long, but they couldn't say if it'd been a day or five days. Surely it hadn't been much longer than that, or there would have been spider webs on some of them, at least.

"Let's head on into Hillsdale," Tucker said, "and see if those three the general told us about are still in town. Maybe these boys went there."

They mounted up and rode back out the way they had come in. They had traveled the road to Hillsdale for about a mile and a half when they saw a place where some wagons had come onto the road. They followed the tracks to a campsite and found where it looked like wagons had been hidden by cut branches, and tracks from horses heading into the hills. "These horse tracks are mixed, some fresh, some not," Tucker said. "We don't know who made them, and I doubt it was those men we followed." He shook his head, frustrated. "Let's get on to Hillsdale, find out what we can, and come back here if we don't get something better to follow. Then we'll see where this trail takes us."

When they got to Hillsdale, they went to the sheriff. He told them three men had come in and were still in town. It was only noon.

CHAPTER 13

BETTER SAFE THAN SORRY

While they were eating their lunch of fresh-caught fish, Thomas Sr. said, "I've got a bad feeling about being here. I think we should leave right away. We shouldn't be close to where those boxes might be found. If anyone sees us, or for some reason tracks those wagons back to our campsite, they'll follow our trail from there up to this lake. We can come back here and go fishing some other time, but right now, we need to put some distance between us and where the wagons were taken from."

Everyone was a little disappointed because they were enjoying themselves, but they knew he was right. They shouldn't be taking any chances. It was decided they would leave right after lunch. They went down the west side of Hillsdale Lake till they came to the road that would take them to Lawrence.

"We should go to Lawrence to throw off anyone who might be tracking us," Tommy said. "Besides, I want to buy a gift for Terry. And when we get there, the drinks in the saloon are on me."

"That's a good idea," Thomas Sr. said. "If anyone is following us, they'll lose the trail in town."

As they approached town, he said, "We should drop the horses off at the blacksmith's and get them all shod. That way, if anyone does trail us from the lake, we won't be making the same tracks to follow to the ranch."

The blacksmith told them he had a helper, but it would take a couple of hours to shoe all of the horses. As the McCoys left the blacksmith and headed down the main street of town, they noticed several newly completed and under construction buildings, and A.C. commented on how fast Lawrence was becoming a city. Tommy stopped at the dress shop and bought a beautiful winter dress and bonnet for Terry, because he was pretty sure she didn't have any nice winter ones. The owner wrapped it into a pretty package for him. The others went to the mercantile and bought some things to take back to the ranch. When they met up on the boardwalk, they decided to go to the hotel restaurant and get something to eat. The fish they had caught were good, but it was the last thing they had eaten, and their stomachs were talking to them.

They also knew they had a couple of hours or more to kill before the horses were ready. They spent about forty-five minutes in the restaurant and figured they had at least another forty-five minutes more, so they decided they would go to the saloon and collect on Tommy's offer to buy the drinks. They all ordered beer, even Jeb, but Thomas Sr. frowned and ordered him a sarsaparilla instead. "You're lucky we even let you come in here," he told him, "and you're definitely not old enough to drink."

As they drank, they talked about going back to the lake and doing some night fishing. When everyone had finished their first round of beer, Tommy said, "Let's get a deck of cards and play a few hands. Does anyone want another drink?"

A.C. looked around at the others and said, "Of course, we all do, especially since you're buying." When Tommy ordered another round, he asked for a deck of cards. They sat at a table by the window, so they could look outside if they wanted to, and played without money or chips, pretending they were betting a minimum of a hundred dollars and had a limit of five thousand on any bet. They had some fun pretending they were rich and could throw away their money in a card game.

After about an hour had passed, Tommy asked Jeb if he would go to the blacksmith and see if the horses were ready. A few minutes later, he returned and said that the blacksmith was on the last horse, and all would be ready in about fifteen minutes. They played a couple more hands and finished their drinks, and then started down the street to fetch the horses. They paid the blacksmith, mounted up, and headed for the ranch.

CHAPTER 14

CATCHING THE ESCAPEES

Back in Hillsdale, the Pinkertons asked the sheriff if he could point the men out to them. "Sure," he said. "I have one of my deputies planted across the street from them."

They left their horses in front of the sheriff's office and walked down the street with him. The men were in the restaurant below the hotel, and the sheriff pointed them out through a window.

"If you'll stay on this side of the street," said Agent Tucker, "we're going to take positions on both ends of the building. I'll send two men around back, just in case they try to slip out that way. We'll wait till they come outside; we don't want any innocent people to be caught up in gunplay, if that's what happens."

"That's fine with me," said the sheriff. "Just make sure you give 'em a chance to surrender. I don't want them shot dead in my town just because they walk out of the restaurant."

"Don't worry, I'll give them a choice," Agent Tucker assured him. "It'll be up to them."

When the men inside finished eating and started for the door, the Pinkertons had stationed three men at each front corner of the building, two by the back door, and the sheriff with his deputy across the street.

As the men came onto the boardwalk, Agent Tucker stepped in front of them out in the street. "Hello, boys," he said. "You're a long way from the Little Osage River."

They seemed startled to hear the name of the place where their hideout had been, and their hands immediately went to their guns.

"Don't do it," Agent Tucker said. "We've got you surrounded, and you're outnumbered three to one."

But the highwaymen's horses were just a few steps away, and they thought if they could get to them, they might have a chance. They pulled their guns, and one of them fired at Tucker while the other two each shot at the corners of the building where they saw the other agents sticking their heads out around the corner of the building. It was a senseless move, and had they known who they were up against, they might not have done it. The Pinkertons were not regular lawmen.

Tucker had jumped behind a horse when the man reached for his gun, and they started shooting. During the melee he stepped out and fired at the man who had tried to shoot him, hitting him square in the chest. The man dropped face first on the steps from the boardwalk and tumbled to the street.

The other two managed to get off one more shot each before the men at the corners of the building cut them down. All three were dead in a couple of seconds.

The sheriff came running over. "Well, you gave them a chance," he said, pushing back his hat to get a better look at them. "If they weren't outlaws, they wouldn't have tried to shoot."

The Pinkertons found the gold in their saddlebags and turned it over to the sheriff. "Someone will be along to claim this," Agent Tucker told him. He held out his hand to shake. "We're going to go head back down the road," he said. "On the way here, we saw another group of highwaymen heading to what looked like a hideout, but by the time we got there, they had cleared out. But we found a place where someone had hidden a couple of wagons, and we're going to see if we can pick up a trail from there."

The sheriff clasped his hand and shook it heartily. "Thanks for your help," Agent Tucker said. "Please let the general know how much gold you have recovered here and if anyone else comes into town spending fifty dollar gold pieces."

"Don't worry," the sheriff said. "I will."

It was after three o'clock when the Pinkertons got to the campsite. They looked around and discovered the place where the horses had been hidden, and then found where several had gone up the hill. It took them about an hour to find where the McCoys had stopped to fish. They followed their trail down the hill to the west of the lake until they came to the road that headed toward Lawrence. They started following the tracks at a quick pace because they knew they only had a couple hours of daylight left, and they didn't want to lose the trail or have to stop for darkness before they found the men.

The sun was dropping from the sky when they reached the turnoff road leading to the McCoys' ranch. Agent Tucker and Cole headed toward the ranch and told the others to keep following the tracks on the road. "We'll meet you in Lawrence!" he said as they parted.

It was just getting dark when they came through the gate of the McCoys' ranch.

CHAPTER 15

SAFE AND SOUND

Tommy and the others had made it to the ranch just as the sun was dropping below the hills. After putting away his horse, Tommy came inside the house with his gift for Terry. When she saw him, she ran to the doorway and squeezed him tightly, hugging him for all she was worth. She was very relieved that they had made it back safe and sound. When she realized that he was only hugging her with one arm, she was afraid that he had been hurt. But when she pulled back from him to check him over, she saw he was holding something behind his back.

"What did you do?" she said, blushing a little as he presented the package. "You shouldn't have!" she exclaimed. He told her to open it, which she did eagerly.

She pulled out the dress and bonnet, touched the soft material, and exclaimed about their beauty. Looking in his eyes, she smiled and gave him a nice kiss. "Thank you," she said, "for noticing that I didn't have a nice winter dress or winter bonnet." She had just gone into the bedroom to put them away when Tommy heard horses outside.

When he went out on the porch, he was surprised to

see the riders were the same Pinkertons who had visited a couple months before. Surely they were going to be asking questions. They dismounted, and Agent Tucker came up the steps of the porch. He identified himself, and Tommy said, "Yeah, I remember you. What brings you down this way again?"

"As you know from my last visit, we've been trailing fifty dollar gold pieces spent from here to Kentucky. We were on our way back here to start looking around again when we were informed of men spending gold pieces in Missouri and Kansas close by the borders. We tracked a few of them down and recovered some of the gold." Tommy nodded, his face expressionless.

"When we got to Pleasanton, we found out from the sheriff that you had helped him take out a gang of highwaymen," Agent Tucker continued. "It's a funny thing that some of you McCoys have been turning up spending gold coins or in the areas where the gold coins were found. A couple of you even managed to find some large gold deposits. I figured I'd stop in and ask what you were doing down there around Pleasanton."

"I'm sorry to hear that you're holding suspicions about us," Tommy said. "As we told you before, my girl's father had some coins left from the sale of their old ranch, and she paid for everything we've done here on the ranch with that, plus paid those who went to Kentucky, but it's all gone now." He folded his arms on his chest.

"A couple of our kinfolk got lucky and got rich. I wish it would've happened before you had started looking for this lost gold. Unfortunately, it didn't, but they still found gold and are now rich because of it. As for us being down around Pleasanton, we were there because my girl's cousin asked us to come and help build a barn. Us McCoys try to help out anyone we can, but if family asks, we do it, no matter how far we have to travel. You can check with Terry's cousin. She'll tell you."

"I'll do just that," said the Pinkerton, "We don't leave loose ends when we're on a case."

And he patted his pockets as if looking for something. "So you got hit by some highwaymen, I take it?" he said. And he pulled out a pipe as if ready to settle in for a story.

Tommy nodded. "When we finished the barn, Terry's cousin gave us some supplies to bring back home as her way of paying us," he said. "We tried to refuse, but they wouldn't hear of it. The first night we camped, a gang of men on horseback came by and took the wagon at gunpoint, as well as all the guns and horses they saw. We were lucky they didn't kill us," he said, shaking his head. "We were also lucky we had a couple of horses hobbled in a meadow away from the campsite. We followed the men's trail, and when we saw where they ended up, we went for the sheriff. He got us our wagon and supplies back and said if he found out there was a bounty on any of those men he'd be getting in contact with the sheriff in Lawrence to let us know we had some money coming as a reward." And Tommy smiled. "In fact, next time I go to town, I was going to ask him. We sure could use some money to get this ranch some livestock."

Agent Tucker put the pipe back in his pocket without lighting it.

"We'll probably be seeing each other again," he said. "But right now, I've got to get back to my men. We're on the trail of some men that looked to be heading into Lawrence," then he turned and stepped off the porch and mounted his horse. "I'll be in touch," he said, and he and his fellow agent rode quickly back in the direction of Lawrence.

Agent Tucker found the rest of his men in Lawrence's only saloon and was told that once it got dark and the horses they had been following had come down the main street, the tracks had blended in with those made by the other horses and wagons that had been going up and down the road during the day. "We'll stay the night and check all the businesses in the morning to see if any strangers had ridden into town," Tucker said. He went over to see the sheriff. Sheriff Banes told him he hadn't noticed any strangers, though it didn't mean someone hadn't passed through in the afternoon, because for most of it, he had been taking a nap. Tucker went to the hotel and got his men rooms for the night.

The next morning, they checked all of the businesses but came up with no new information. When he sent word to the general, he got back a message telling him to investigate reports of gold coins spent in Ottawa, Kansas, and Harrisonville, Missouri. He told his men to get ready to ride back to Hillsdale again, but there, they would split into two groups; he'd take three men to Harrisonville, and the other five would go to Ottawa. "I want to stop once more at the McCoys'," he said. "I have a couple more questions for them."

It was early afternoon when they came once again to the McCoys' ranch.

Tommy was in the barn when they rode down the lane. "Back so soon? What can I help you with?" he said.

Tucker didn't get off his horse. "I was wondering, what happened to all of the men that you had working here before?" he said. "I guess they're gone, because you don't have nearly as many horses in that corral of yours as you did."

"Well," Tommy said, "it's a hard life out here. We tried to help the men who wanted to ranch alongside of us, and Lord knows they worked hard." He took off his hat, smoothed his hair, and put the hat back on again. "Unfortunately, they could barely scratch out a living. We couldn't pay wages to the ones who stayed here to work for us, just food and a place to sleep, so most of them decided to see if they had a better chance somewhere else. Some went back to where their homes had been before the war, in Virginia and Tennessee." (He said this, knowing quite well they had gone to California, Montana, the Dakotas and probably Ohio.)

"One of our kinfolk in Kentucky, one of those that struck it rich, sent everyone a little bit of money, a loan to help us out, and they thought it was best if they tried to leave while they had the funds to do it."

The Pinkerton's face was impassive, "Well," he said, "I've got to check out some more places those gold coins were spent, and since I'm going down that way, I'm going to check out your story with your girl's cousin, just to make sure everything ties in, like you say."

Tommy nodded. "If you find her, she'll tell you what I told you; we were there to help build their barn, and that's it. When we got it done, we headed for home, and that's when those robbers hit us."

"Well," Agent Tucker said, "if what you say is true, I doubt I'll be coming back this way, so y'all take care, and hopefully, we won't be seeing each other again."

• • •

When the Pinkertons got to Hillsdale, Tucker and three others went to Harrisonville, and the other five went to Ottawa. They arrived in Ottawa before their leader got to Harrisonville and found out from the sheriff that three men had come through town a couple days before and spent a few coins. They wired the general to see if they had any other reports, but none had come in yet, then sent a wire to Harrisonville, telling Agent Tucker what they had found and that they were waiting for instructions.

When Tucker and his men rode into Harrisonville, they went to see the sheriff. "There were two men who came through a couple of days ago but didn't stay," Sheriff Spencer told them, "and they spent a couple of gold coins. If you're looking for gold coins, you might go to the church and ask our pastor. He had a huge donation back in May, which he divided up among needy folks. He also gave a bunch to the town."

They found the church they'd been directed to was empty, so they approached the little house next to it. As they reached the front porch, the pastor came outside. "Hello, gentlemen," he said. "What can I do you for?"

"Pastor," said Agent Tucker, "we're from the Pinkerton detective agency, and we're trying to track down some gold coins. The sheriff told us that you had a big donation back in May. Can you tell me anything about it?"

"Sure," the pastor said. "One day, I came outside and there were all these boxes, strongboxes, as I think they call them. They were stacked next to the church. I don't know who it was that left them." This was actually the truth. He never had asked their names, and the storeroom was by the church. He just didn't add the part about the donors helping him put the boxes into his house.

"When I got one of them open, I saw all this money— more money than I had ever dreamed I would see in my life. I got scared at first, but then I saw the note the donor had left. I'll never forget what it said: 'These spoils of war should go to the innocent families who lost their homes, ranches, and loved ones in the war. I'd like the church to see that those in need get as much help as possible, and also give a good portion to the City Hall for town redevelopment and programs for those in need.'"

"Then, at the bottom, in big letters, it was printed, GOD WILL KNOW HOW YOU DISBURSE THESE FUNDS. I'll never forget that letter for as long as I live." And he swallowed hard, as if working to compose himself.

"I went to the mayor, and he said to wait a couple of months and see if anyone came to claim it. We did, and when no one came, I started giving out the money to do what the letter said, help people start their lives over. As the note advised, I gave a good portion to City Hall. They set up low-interest loan programs for people and a charity fund we helped them create. And they did some rebuilding to the town as well—built a new bridge over the creek yonder and replaced the whole boardwalk on the left side of Main Street. They still have a little bit left, but most of it has been given out in the form of charity from the church and grant credit from the bank. That's where I deposited most of the money, and they dished it out to those with the proper papers to receive it." The pastor looked at the agents in front of him, as if daring them to challenge the good use of the disputed coins.

"Basically, Agent Tucker," he said, "I gave away all but a small sum, which I kept as an emergency fund for the church."

"Well, just how much gold was there?" asked Agent Tucker.

"I think there were seventy boxes or so. Can't recall exactly."

Agent Tucker blinked hard. "Pastor," he said, "I thank you for letting me know about this. I appreciate your honesty." And the Pinkerton agents took their leave.

It seemed that they had found out where most of the gold had ended up. Tucker went to the telegraph office and sent a wire to the general, telling him about the pastor and the donation. While there, he received the wire from his men, so he sent another wire to the general, asking what he wanted them to do. The general's reply said that the information they had gathered could account for a little more than half of the gold, so they were to wait where they were and see if they got any additional reports of men spending coins. They were to wait a week, and if they got no further information, they were to go back to Lawrence.

At the end of the week, a wire came, saying suspicious men had come through Wichita, Kansas, and there were reports of coins being spent in Jefferson City, Missouri. During that week, Agent Tucker had sent a wire to Pleasanton, asking Sheriff Cole to contact Terry's cousin and verify their story, which he did, sending back a wire saying she told him they had come down to help build her barn. Satisfied that the McCoys were not involved, he resigned himself to returning to the trail of spent coins.

Back at the ranch, the McCoys got a letter from Terry's cousin, telling them that the Pinkertons had asked the sheriff to verify their story. While relieved that the Pinkertons probably wouldn't be back, they still knew they couldn't risk spending any of the gold for several years. And so they decided that everyone would pitch in the three thousand Wiley had sent each of them and the five hundred that came from the bounties they received from the sheriff of Pleasanton to buy all the cattle and horses they could raise to sell. They decided they could even safely mix in some of their gold when they made deposits from the sales. All would be partners in the livestock business, getting equal shares of the profits. With this new plan, everyone began feeling good about their lives and futures again.

Especially Tommy and Terry. Terry couldn't wait to see her man coming back home from work on the ranch each day; she enjoyed having supper ready for him, holding him close, and feeling everything was right again. But really, it was the part after supper that she really looked forward to, when they went into the bedroom and she was able to do much more than just hold him. She was trying to make up for all the time they'd lost. Terry told him and anyone who'd listen that she was going to marry her man this time, and he wasn't going anywhere without her.

Tommy couldn't have been any happier with the way things had turned out with the Pinkertons and couldn't have asked God for anything better than returning his beloved Terry's heart to him. His life was fulfilled, as far as he was concerned.

The Pinkertons were searching far and wide for any

news of gold coins turning up, investigating every lead. And as for what happened to the McCoys who escaped to California, Montana, and the Dakota's, they ran into some problems along their journeys. Unfortunately for them, opening up the possibility of being tracked down. Will they ever be able to live and feel safe? Well, that's in the next sagas of *The McCoys: Before the Feud* series.

You're Invited To...

As you sit here reading this you might have thought about how much others would enjoy this book as much as you have. If you'd love to share that enjoyment with others then would you leave a review?

www.TheMcCoysBeforeTheFeud.com/review

ALSO BY THOMAS MCCOY
IN THE *MCCOYS BEFORE THE FEUD* SERIES

Before The Feud (Book 1)

A corrupt general. A stockpile of plundered Southern riches. Can a proud family reclaim the gold for its rightful owners?

Kansas-Missouri border, 1865. Tommy McCoy burns for justice. Reeling from the end of the bloody Civil War, he learns that a corrupt Northern general has raided the bounty of the Confederacy and plans to keep it. Tommy and his shrewd father vow to get back the valuables for innocent Southern families or die trying.

With time running out before the general's reinforcements arrive, Tommy risks a deadly confrontation in a series of secret raids. Can he secure the rightful Confederate property before the North deals the McCoys a final crushing blow?

The McCoys: Before the Feud is the first book in a deeply-researched historical Western saga. If you like dusty battles, a different point of view on yesteryear, and twists you won't see coming, then you'll love Thomas A. McCoy's gripping tale of justice for the people.

Buy *The McCoys: Before the Feud* to join a family's quest for justice today!

Home To Kentucky (Book 2)

A treacherous journey. Wagons packed with gold. Will the McCoys outrun a group of lawmen or swing from the gallows?

Kansas, 1865. Wiley McCoy can't wait to return home. He counts down the days until his family can stop laying low and return to Kentucky with the rightfully plundered valuables they took back for the South. But crossing the open prairie with four wagons full of gold may bring Wiley a lethal set of new problems.

With desperate outlaws and opportunistic deserters at every turn, Wiley and the other McCoys must watch their backs to survive. But they never expected their greatest enemy to come in the form of ten brilliant Pinkerton detectives…

Can Wiley make it home before the lawmen slip a rope around his neck?

Home to Kentucky is the second book in The McCoys: Before the Feud saga of historical Western novels. If you like determined heroes, realistic Southern settings, and quests for justice, then you'll love Thomas A. McCoy's treacherous wagon ride.

Buy *Home to Kentucky* to ride along with the McCoys today!

ABOUT THE AUTHOR

Thomas Allan McCoy is the author of the Western Historical Fiction series The McCoy's: Before the Feud. As a direct descendant of the original McCoy family that was involved in the legendary feud between the Hatfields and McCoys, he provides a unique perspective and valuable insights regarding their traits, morals, and how family honor affected the way they carried out their lives after the Civil War. Inspired by the dramatic events that occurred within his own family history, McCoy weaves together facts and fiction to bring to life events that were happening in our country before this timeless feud from the 1860s took place.

McCoy's father, grandfather, great, and great, great grandfather were all born in Pikeville, Kentucky. However, he grew up in Southern California. In addition to writing, McCoy loves fishing, traveling, and baseball. He now lives in Arizona with his wife.